THE SERMON THAT LED TO MURDER

Rev. Malcolm G. Lorimer

Max Books

First published in the UK in 2019 by Max Books

A CIP catalogue record for this title is available
from the British Library

ISBN: 978-0-9562224

Typeset by Andrew Searle
Cover illustration by Bob Bond

Printed and bound by RLH Print Ltd

MAX BOOKS
2 Newbold Way
Nantwich Cheshire CW5 7AX
Tel: 01270 625278
Email: maxcricket@btinternet.com

Chapter One

The story begins in the 1960's on a hot summer's day.

ELEGANT AND beautiful the butterfly flew around the vicarage garden, on this lazy, hazy summer afternoon. Its wings an extraordinary kaleidoscope of colours and patterns seemed to exemplify the day. The sun glinting on the greenhouse, the air heavy with the scent of summer and at last the butterfly came to rest on the brim of a straw panama hat.

It was the hat of Rev Charles Jowett and he was slumbering in the vicarage garden and all seemed at peace with the world.

What the butterfly had not noticed, but maybe it had and didn't care was the trickle of blood that seeped from underneath the straw boater and made it's way in a crimson ribbon down the vicar's cheek.

The butterfly may not have noticed it but Heather, his wife certainly did as she came out into the garden carrying a tray with glasses and a large jug of iced Pimm's. Her scream pierced the air and the butterfly was gone, the tray crashing on the concrete flags, glass, ice cubes and fruit juice cascading down the steps.

Everything then happened quickly, the next door neighbour came running into the garden, the 999 call, the attempts trying to resuscitate, people standing around feeling helpless. A few minutes later, it felt a lot longer, the loud sirens blared in the quiet lanes and heralded arrival of an ambulance and a police car. But it was too late, the vicar was dead.

At first glance it seemed he had fallen in the vicarage garden against the rockery, there was evidence of blood on one of the stones and Charles' clothes had soil on them. There was a cut on the side of his head, a long gash above his ear. It looked as if he had fallen and tried to sit back in the chair, he obviously passed out and the pool of blood underneath the chair, evidence for how long he must have been there.

Heather had been taken inside and was distraught, a few neighbours surrounded her and then the curate arrived, Rev. Rory Coverdale.

Eventually the neighbours melted away, the ambulance took away the lifeless body of the Rev Charles Jowett and the police made their exit saying they would be back in the morning.

Heather sat in the chair in the study, her eyes were glazed, she was looking vacantly ahead of her, not focusing on anything just an empty expression on her face.

Rory was at the other side of the room looking out into the garden. Heather repeated the words she had said all afternoon. "I don't understand, how could it have happened? I was in the house, surely I would have heard him if he had fallen."

Rory turned and looked at her sympathetically, "That's what the police say, he fell and hit his head, it must have made him groggy and disorientated, he didn't realise he had hurt himself so much. He probably lost consciousness and then you found him."

"How long had he been there?" Heather was now wringing her hands.

"You can't blame yourself, Heather, it was an accident." Rory tried to console her.

"But I do, if I hadn't been at the other side of the house cleaning that spare room I could have helped him, maybe even saved his life. What a waste."

The doorbell rang and Rory answered, the quick footsteps on the hall floor of a women's shoes were heard.

The door burst open and a rather large and older version of Heather came into the room.

"Heather, I came as soon as I could...what on earth has happened..."

It was Heather's sister Joyce and now she was here Rory made his excuses and left saying that he would inform the Bishop and look after things in the parish, Heather was not to be troubled by anything.

As Rory walked back to his flat at the other side of the village his steps were heavy and his eyes downcast, looking at the pavement and he hoped he would get home without meeting anyone. What an awful thing to have happened, and after so much that was going well in the Parish, it was so tragic, so senseless, poor Heather. It was now raining quite heavily and Rory saw it as somehow appropriate as he trudged back to his flat down the lanes of the small country village of Little Stanbury.

Chapter Two

YOU HAVE to go back a few weeks to understand what happened at St. Stephen's Parish Church to fully comprehend the tragic events that occurred in the vicarage garden.

Rev. Charles Jowett was in his early fifties, an Anglican clergyman of the middle of the road variety, although his early days were strongly influenced by the Catholic wing of the church. He had wondered if he should join the Roman Catholic Church at one time but then after college his views and leanings swung back to the centre of the church. He was a very good clergyman, conciseness and diligent, his ministry wouldn't set the world on fire but it would sustain and help many people.

He was sitting with his wife Heather having breakfast, in the Vicarage, he seemed rather excited and Heather was puzzled.

"Do you know Heather, I believe this Sunday's sermon will be one of the best I have ever preached."

Heather paused and lowered the paper she was reading and looked at her husband quizzically over her glasses. "What makes you say that dear?" she was puzzled.

"I feel it in my bones, I have not had such confidence in a sermon for a long time, people will sit up and take note, mark my words."

Heather resumed reading the paper.

"I hope so dear."

She dearly hoped he would not be disappointed, good vicar that he was, he was not the world's best preacher but he tried so hard, perhaps too hard.

She confided to the curate Rory Coverdale her fears before the Sunday in question.

"I do hope Charles doesn't get too disappointed, he puts so much effort into his sermons and yet gets so little response."

Rory thought that Charles' sermons were good but these days people don't put as much store by them as they used to do in the past.

Heather was younger than Charles. She had been brought up a Methodist. As the daughter of a Methodist Minister she had moved around the country quite a bit as she was growing up. It had given her an easy way of getting on with people and she had a very open nature, she jogged and kept fit with karate and Yoga and although their budget didn't stretch too far she had an eye for fashions which suited and complemented her. She chose clothes which made her look younger, not for Heather the frumpy woollen twin-sets worn by the ladies of the Mothers Union. She had met Charles at a retreat centre which she was managing. He had come once or twice to visit and then his visits got more frequent as their friendship blossomed and they were married seven years ago. They had no children but were very happy with one another. Heather was vivacious and good company.

Sunday arrived and Charles seemed to have a new air about him, he seemed confident and looked ready to confront the world.

The sermon was very different to his usual ones.

He was forceful, direct, people shifted in their pews uncomfortably, they looked down at their hymn books afraid to catch the vicar's eye. Charles had chosen to preach about the way confession was both good for the soul and also how it helped a person face up to issues of guilt. How our past can weigh us down and if there are things that have happened which have not been resolved how they can affect us today. Heather had never heard Charles preach with such conviction and it seemed he certainly had the wind of the Spirit inspiring him and driving him on.

The congregation of St. Stephen's had also never heard the like of this sermon before. They were used to more stodgy fare and it was as if they were suddenly presented with a gourmet banquet when they had come prepared for beans on toast. But the taste of the fare was not very appetising to some. The sermon challenged the hearers to look at themselves in a way few had ever done so before. There were touches of John Wesley and Billy Graham in the address and a few sobs and the use of handkerchiefs were on open display.

At the end of the sermon there was a silence. It was a strange silence and one which seemed as profound as the sermon. No-one moved and then one person began to clap, it was like a cascade as clapping and then laughter broke out around the church. People began to stand up and the clapping echoed around the small Norman Church.

The congregation had never heard a sermon like it. The hearers congratulated Charles on the way out, not their usual, 'nice service vicar', or 'good hymns today'. People were visibly moved, tears in their eyes, a few women with handkerchiefs held to their faces. Even Heather was taken aback, she certainly had never heard Charles preach like that before, confident and challenging as the sermon really hit home. It also seemed to take something out of him, after a light lunch he was asleep and didn't waken till after five, just in time to get ready for evensong.

There was a dissenter though, old Wilfrid, the former church-warden. He had shaken his head as he came out of church that morning. "Nay Vicar, tha's stirred up a reight hornet's nest this morning, no good will come of it-best let sleeping dogs lie, leave those things in the past."

In the following days there were many phone calls from parishioners and also there were the visitors to the vicarage.

Chapter Three

THE FIRST visitor was the church-warden, the Colonel. Charles thought it was just a routine visit about church affairs, little did he realise what a chain of events his sermon had started.

The sharp rat-a-tat heralded the arrival of Charles' visitor. The Colonel was tall, thin and lithe. He had a military bearing and without knowing anything about him, you would have guessed he had been in the army. His wife had died five years previously and he had thrown himself into working in the village, as church warden and also on various committees. His organization of the yearly Remembrance Day parade was first-class and it was organised with a military precision and care which took weeks of preparation and thought. He would lead the procession, with his beret, blazer, a row of medals on his chest, barking out the orders to the small group of scouts and brownies who by the time they had been in a couple of processions knew the importance of keeping in step. A small band also was present and when the Colonel said the famous words, 'At the going down of the sun we will remember them', a lone bugler playing the last post, there was not a dry eye amongst the assembled throng around the war memorial.

The Colonel marched into the study and promptly sat down in the chair opposite the desk, leaving Charles a little perplexed and quite taken aback, he realised that this was a conversation he was not in control over. Before Charles had time to take his seat, the Colonel began.

"I will come straight to the point vicar, damned good sermon last Sunday, just what the troops needed."

The description of the parish congregation of St Stephen's as troops made Charles smile and think how incongruous it was, but then that is how the Colonel would think.

"Would you like a drink Colonel, I know it is early in the day but..."

"Whiskey would be fine, make mine a double, I think I will need it. And get yourself one you'll need it after listening to what I have to say."

Charles poured two large whiskeys smiling to himself as he did so, after being given permission in his own house to pour a drink.

He handed a glass to the Colonel and resumed his seat.

The Colonel took a large gulp and sat back in his chair looking keenly at the vicar.

"What I am about to tell you vicar not a soul in the world knows about, I have never told anyone, not even my wife when she was alive. I need to know before I begin if I can trust you, can I vicar?"

Charles took a small sip of the whiskey and looked directly at the Colonel. "Yes, you can trust me, I know about listening to people's stories and keeping confidentiality, you can rely on me Colonel."

The Colonel looked relieved and for the first time smiled. "I knew you are a good man vicar and I could trust you. What I am about to tell you may alter our relationship though and there may be further consequences."

Charles looked thoughtful, wondering what on earth he was about to hear.

The Colonel took another large gulp and Charles quickly rose and re-filled his glass.

The Colonel's eyes narrowed and he seemed to be casting his mind back to events that happened a long time ago.

"As you know vicar, I have served all my life in the Army. I joined up before the Second World War and when the war started I was a Captain in the Royal Lancashire Fusiliers. You could say I had a good war or a lucky war depending on how you saw it. I rose to become a Colonel and saw service in France and then after Dunkirk went with the allied forces on D Day. You have to see that this was my life, I didn't expect to come back alive, so many of my friends and comrades had fallen around me. War is a strange thing vicar, it's like another world where the rules are different and if you get it wrong you pay with your life.

Anyway, we landed at D Day on Sword beach and fought our way forward. I was leading a small group of about twenty men and we were going to take out a machine gun post at the top of a hill overlooking the beach. It was a difficult one because it was well fortified and under a rock overhang, the perfect place to observe the beach and it was causing us a lot of damage, it had to be taken out. I had a number two Pete Saunders, brave as a lion and although he had little education, brought up in the back streets of Gateshead if I remember, I would have no other man at my side in the thick of battle. We were pinned down by the machine gun post and couldn't move forward, we lost a couple of men and it was becoming hopeless. We fell back and re-grouped to decide what to do. Pete suggested we go at it from either side at once. It seemed a good idea and he led one group and I led the other. We got close before opening up together and let them have it, the 'full monty,' machine-guns, hand grenades, we gave it all we had. We took a terrible toll though, they mowed us down and all looked lost until Pete who had fallen and I thought he was wounded suddenly got up and rushed them straight on with his machine-gun blazing. I saw what was happening and got up and followed him. He took that post single handed and by the time I was close I could see they were all dead in the machine gun post with Peter Saunders standing over them with his machine gun. It was then I tripped and fell forward, my gun went off and I couldn't believe what happened next, Pete Saunders collapsed, a bullet through his back. He was dead. I just stood over him, stunned, when a couple of soldiers came by and saw the scene. They congratulated me on the capture of the machine-gun post. Before I could say anything a shell went off and that was the last thing I knew until I woke up in a military hospital in Kent a few days later.

My memory was hazy and although I was injured it wasn't too serious, I remember an officer coming to see me and saying I was quite a hero, I didn't understand it, I thought they must have mixed me up with someone else.

During the following weeks I got my memory back but by then they had pinned a medal on me and I was the hero who had taken the machine gun post single-handed. I tried to play it down but no-one would listen. I was too ashamed to tell the truth, so I let it go on. I honestly thought I would be going back to the front-line and I would be dead anyway in a couple of months, what would it matter?

I did go back to the front-line but I suppose as they say I had a lucky war and although I was always putting myself in dangerous situations, I always managed to survive .When the war ended I stayed in the Army and rose to the rank of Colonel before I retired.

The rest you know vicar, I settled here in the village and played the part of the village Colonel. The war hero who wasn't, I threw myself into raising money for war charities and also in the last few years as you know I have been your church warden.

Vicar, I feel a complete sham. For most of my life I have lived a lie and kept it all to myself. Your sermon made me realise I had to be honest and tell someone. Now I have and feel a bit better but also I am ashamed of myself. If you want me to resign as church warden you shall have my letter in the morning."

Charles drained the last whiskey and looked into the bottom of the glass reflectively.

"Thank you for telling me your story, Colonel, it must have taken great courage and I respect you for it.

I don't think your resigning will accomplish anything. If it helps I think more of you now because you have had the courage to tell me your story."

The Colonel sat hunched up wringing his hands. "How can you say that, I have been living as a fraud for so long, people look at me in the village and see the brave Colonel, decorated with his medals, if only they knew."

"You know" said Charles "War is a strange time, men do brave acts and also foolish ones. The normal rules of life are suspended, we kill people and call it bravery. Life is not black and white in wartime there are always shades of grey."

"You can philosophise vicar but I know what I am and I don't like it. What can I do?"

Charles looked at him, thoughtfully. "I am not sure, I have not got a quick and easy answer but what you have done today is the first step and that's very important. I would like to think and pray about it all and talk further when I have found an answer."

The Colonel rose from his chair and shook the vicar's hand. "You know vicar, I was right to tell you, thank you for that sermon, I needed to tell my story, I have held it back too long. I must now face the future and it's consequences, whatever they are."

With that he turned and left the vicarage, marching down the path as if to a distant drum.

Charles returned to his study and poured himself another whiskey and sat in his chair. For a long time his mind was going over the story he had just heard and wondering what help or guidance he could give.

Chapter Four

THE FOLLOWING day Charles had another visitor, an occasional member of the congregation, a retired solicitor and local benefactor, Peter Frobisher.

He was a little red-faced man with balding hair. He wore glasses which made his narrow eyes squint giving him the appearance of a little animal which did not like the daylight. He also had a nervous laugh which he used to chuckle at his own jokes, few that they were. He was the village benefactor, few organisations had not benefited from his largesse whilst he had lived in the village, from the cricket club to the luncheon club for the elderly, and the church. His generosity it seemed knew no bounds, a retired solicitor his practice must have been a good one to keep him and a wife whose lavish tastes in clothes and jewellery not to mention the exotic holidays were tolerated by the village as long as the donations continued.

Peter Frobisher came into the study his eyes squinting at the light and looking more like a frightened mole than usual.

"Please sit down Peter, Can I offer you a drink?"

"No, no it's alright I want to come straight to the point if I may vicar."

Charles lent forward a little in his chair, wondering if this had anything to do with last Sunday's sermon.

Peter began hesitantly……"Vicar…I have rarely heard a sermon like the one you preached last

Sunday...it was the like of which I have never heard before."

Charles felt embarrassed. "Well, I know it was a bit different, I suppose I felt inspired to preach it."

"Inspired. Yes, that what it was, you have never preached better, vicar."

"Well thank you Peter. I really appreciate your comments."

It was obvious that Peter Frobisher was not finished and there was something else he wanted to say, but it was taking a time for him to pluck up enough courage to say it.

"You see vicar....that sermon moved me... it pricked my conscience...it made me think of something in my life which I have never told to anyone before but I feel I must tell you about it."

Charles looked amazed. "Well I'm humbled by your confidence in me and of course anything you tell me will be held in the strictest confidence."

"Of course.....could I have that drink, I think I may need it..."

"Yes of course". Charles got up and went to the cabinet.

"What would you like? A beer or some spirits?"

"A brandy if you have it please."

Charles raised his eyebrows to himself as he poured Peter a large brandy and poured himself a tonic water.

As he resumed his seat he saw Peter take a gulp of the brandy and then as if it had oiled the wheels began what was to become a remarkable story.

"What I am about to tell you vicar, could ruin me, I have kept it to myself for many years but now after your sermon I feel that I have to tell someone."

He took another drink from the glass.

"As you know I have been solicitor for most of my working life. I started in a country practice in a small market town in Norfolk. As the junior solicitor I was given the routine work, wills, divorces, land conveyances etc. One day there was a death of a Miss Florence Merryweather and I had to execute the will. It was very simple, she had little money and only a modest cottage and few valuable possessions. When I read the will I realised there would be one problem, she didn't seem to have any relatives, and when she had made the will she left everything to her sister who had died a few years before. We advertised of course locally and also in the London Gazette but no relatives came forward. It was my task to go through the papers at the house and they were all in a bureau. There was little of value, but there was what looked like a seaman's wooden chest with some papers which looked like the details and accounts of an old tobacconists shop. I brought the chest back to the office thinking that I would check out the papers and put it in the vault. Eventually the house was sold and all the bills paid and even then we could find no relatives so reluctantly we had to send the money raised to the Crown. I always begrudge doing this, I think the person would never want this to happen and if only they had specified a local charity or something. The chest remained in the vault and it was always something I was going to get round to doing, to sort through the papers and get rid of the chest. It became a bit of a joke in the office. "Miss Merryweather's chest" When were we going to do something about it? But we never did, it sat there for years, until, well, we had a new senior partner and one day he went down to the vault and the next thing we heard was a loud bang and a lot of expletives. He had of course fallen over the box. When he came back up the stairs he asked who was responsible for that 'bloody box' and would they please get rid of it forthwith.

Later that afternoon I went down to the vault and started going through the papers, they were as I thought just the accounts from a business I presumed Miss Merryweather's father had in the town many years before. There was nothing of value and little of historical interest. I decided I would put the papers back into the chest and send it to the local auction, the sea chest would at least fetch a few pounds and the accounts were of local interest. It was when I'd emptied the box that I noticed a strange thing. The inside looked very small when you considered the size of the box on the outside. I examined it carefully and turned it over and even measured the inside, and yes the inside was some six inches smaller that it should have been.

I looked all around the chest but could find nothing until I saw a small groove hidden by a side panel and when the panel was pushed sideways it opened to reveal a drawer which ran the length of the bottom of the box. Inside were dozens of yellowing papers. I examined them and they were share certificates, old ones all from the 1920's with what sounded like very strange names on them. There were lots of them, the names on them I couldn't recognise and there were 'rights issues', 'share splits', 'placing's' and suchlike things I had never heard of, a mountain of paperwork.

I heard the senior partner coming down the steps. I suppose that was the first thing I did which was wrong. I quickly put the certificates back in the drawer and closed it up. When he reached me he surveyed the box and the accounts of the small tobacconists.

'Why on earth have we been keeping this Peter? Get rid of it will you'

'What shall I do with the money if I sent it auction?'

'Give it to a local charity, just get rid of it.'

With that he turned, climbed the stairs and went out of the offices leaving me alone with the chest.

I opened the drawer again and took out all the certificates and took them upstairs and put them in a locked drawer in my desk.

The following day I bought a copy of The Financial Times, much to the surprise of my wife who knew I didn't take much interest in such matters.

I scanned the names of the stocks and shares but could find none of the ones I had seen the previous afternoon, the contents of Miss Merryweather's chest. I put the paper down, disappointed and thought nothing more about it.

Later that week we sent Miss Merryweather's chest to the local auction house and it made a few pounds which we put in the charity account.

That was that, I thought little more about it until a few months later and a new member Gary arrived at my golf club and as Membership Secretary I had to interview him and take down his details.

He was a stockbroker, selling stocks and shares and as soon as he said this I remembered the certificates I had in my desk.

I asked him if he would take a look at some old share certificates from a client of mine, would he be discreet? They may be worthless but my client just wanted to check them out. Gary readily agreed and I took them round to him the following day.

It was two days later while I was in my office that I received the phone call which would change my life. It was from Gary and he sounded very excited.

'Those certificates you gave me, does your client know what they are?'

'I assured him that they didn't.'

'Well,' said Gary, 'You had better prepare them for a shock. They are all old mining shares, Australian and South African, mostly, of companies that don't exist now as they have been taken over. But the shares are still valid and they are still worth something.'

'How much?' I tried to appear casual in my question.

Gary took a deep breath. 'About three and a half million pounds.'

My mouth went dry and I found it difficult to speak. Gary went babbling on asking if he could handle any sale and promising confidentially and could he meet my client. I thanked him and said I would pass on his message. I sat there in the office just staring into space, dumbfounded, what was I to do?

I was faced with a tremendous dilemma. If I said anything to anyone I would have to open Miss Merryweather's file and search again for relatives, this time there would be a succession of gold diggers and charlatans who would come forward as bogus relatives and have to be checked and eliminated. If no-one is found the money would go the Crown. I would also be in trouble from the Law Society and with my partner for not disclosing the certificates earlier. That night I had little sleep. I didn't know what to do.

You have to believe me vicar, what I did next was not just for my benefit but to help others."

Charles took a drink of the tonic water and wished he had poured himself a brandy.

Peter went on. "I told Gary to sell the shares and give me a cheque which I would put in the clients account ready to pass on to my fictitious client.

That is what he did and a few days later there sitting in a bank account which I alone had sole control of was three and a half million pounds."

Charles took another gulp and remained silent.

Peter went on. "Rightly or wrongly I decided to use the money for the benefit of others. I did spend some of money on myself I have to admit. I bought out my partner in the practice and my wife and I bought a new house."

"How did you explain the money to your wife and friends?"

"I said the firm had done very well and also that I had a bequest from a long lost relative."

"I was careful not to be too showy just the occasional extra holiday and a few presents, a different car and a better house. But of course there were the gifts to others. The only organisation I knew Miss Merryweather belonged to was the local Methodist Church. I gave them £30,000 in cash. The money was stuffed in a brown envelope and put through the door of the Minister one night. It was a good job he was an honest man."

Charles smiled to himself and gave thanks for honest clergymen.

"It was quite a sensation in the local newspaper after they had received this anonymous gift. There were also other anonymous gits to various charities. I began to enjoy it. Your church has benefited vicar; remember the fund for the steeple and the restoration of the bells?"

Charles remembered only too well, a big project for the church and a £25,000 anonymous cash donation which arrived at the church one day.

"You see vicar I have been using the money well, what else could I do? And I will continue giving money away, I don't intend to stop, you have to believe me. After your sermon I thought I wanted to tell someone about it, I needed to tell you and get it off my chest."

Peter sat back in chair and looked pleadingly at Charles.

Charles thought for a few moments.

"What you have told me Peter is a remarkable story and one which I find difficult to come to a quick answer to and advice for you. I need to think and pray about it for a time."

"You won't tell anyone will you?" There was a hint of fear in his voice.

"No, you can be rest assured your secret is safe with me. I believe strongly in the confessional and keeping confidences."

Peter looked relieved. "Thank you vicar."

Charles got up from his chair. "I will think and pray about it for a few days and contact you next week."

"Thank you vicar, I knew I could rely on you, you know I already feel a bit better after sharing something which I have kept to myself for so many years, and has been such a burden."

A rather comfortable one thought Charles as he showed Peter out of the house and then returned to the study, poured himself a whisky and sat in a chair thinking for a long time.

The next few days Heather thought Charles looked very thoughtful and she wondered what was worrying him. Every time she got near the subject, Charles brushed her away and changed the subject.

She was used to him having things he could not discuss with her and she gave up trying with a resigned air.

Chapter Five

LATER THAT week Charles, asked pointedly if Heather was going out to her weekly Yoga class that afternoon. Yes, she was and why was he asking she wondered. She didn't bother asking him, she just wished he would give her more respect and take her into his confidence.

After lunch Heather left for the Yoga and Charles went into his study. After about half-an hour the doorbell rang and Charles opened the door and standing before him was the tall statuesque figure of Lady Sara Hetherington. She looked every bit 'The Lady' Charles thought as he ushered her into the study and was glad that he had tidied up a bit and there wasn't too much clutter around. Lady Sara was wearing what looked like an expensive light blue outfit with a matching silk scarf. Charles motioned for her to sit down and he asked if she would like something to drink. She politely refused and looked at Charles demurely obviously finding it very difficult to speak.

"Vicar.... I wanted to see you.... ...."

Charles smiled and tried to put her at her ease.

With high cheekbones and a natural complexion she had olive shaped eyes which she used to great effect. She could have easily been a model in her early days and still had the poise and bearing of one who knew how both to dress and carry herself to great effect.

"It was after your sermon last Sunday." Charles

heart sank. Not another person affected by that sermon, the first wave of elation about the sermon had quickly abated and now he seemed to be engulfed by other people's problems which he could do little about.

"I was really moved by that sermon vicar, it was something I had never heard before and it struck a deep chord within me."

"I'm glad you liked it, I did feel rather strange preaching it, and I'm not sure where the words came from."

"Well, they certainly had an effect on me and I want to tell you something about my life but first I must know that what I am about to tell you will not go any further."

Charles looked concerned. "You have my full assurance Lady Sara that what you say here will be treated in the strictest confidence and it will be like the confessional.

Lady Sara looked re-assured. "Thank you vicar, I thought you would say that. I think I would like a drink after all, do you have a gin and tonic?."

Charles went to the drinks cabinet and poured out two glasses, he thought he may need a drink; it could be a long afternoon.

Lady Sara took a sip and began to speak, now with a renewed confidence.

"As you know vicar I have been married to Sir Thomas for ten years now and we have been very happy. You married us in the church and I thank you for that as it was Sir Thomas second marriage after his divorce from his first wife.

Charles remembered it well. He had to get the permission of the Bishop to be able to conduct the marriage. Sir Thomas had been married for over twenty five years and they had two grown up daughters. Charles had never met his first wife; they had been separated for a number of years and then finally divorced. The Bishop had given special permission and it was one of the first marriages of a divorcee that Charles had conducted.

Lady Sara continued. "We have been so happy these ten years and the girls seemed to have accepted me very well, the only cloud is the illness of Sir Thomas and as you know he has not responded well to treatment in the last few months and he is struggling and I must admit I don't know how much longer he will be able to fight against this terrible disease."

Charles knew only too well the prognosis was not good and he had visited Sir Thomas both in hospital and at home in the last few months. Last Sunday was the first time he had managed to get to church in a long time.

"It is not about Sir Thomas why I am here. It is about me." Lady Sara took another sip of the gin which seemed to give her more confidence to continue.

"I want to tell you a story which I hope won't shock you but you need to hear it and I need to tell someone."

Charles lent back in his chair little knowing what he was about to hear.

"I was born and grew up in London. It was the fifties when I was in my teens. I wanted to be a model, Carnaby Street and Mary Quant, that's all I could think about.

Charles looked at her and thought even in her fifties she had the look and the poise of a model. He could imagine how beautiful she would have been in her younger days.

It was a wild time and I was in the middle of it all, parties, drugs, pop groups, the life of a model. Life seemed to be something to be grasped there and then, there was little thought of the future or consequences of any actions. I was dating a singer in a pop group. They made a hit single and we all took off to Barbados, about 15 of us for a wild ten days. I don't remember much about it, I was either drunk or high as a kite on drugs, but I do remember something. Vic that was his name, he was a real romantic, he had never really grown up and he said he was madly in love with me. I wasn't sure about anything, and the drugs and drink just made things somehow not real. It was like I was walking through a dream, it was colourful and beautiful but it was not reality. On the third day there he said he wanted to marry me. I went along with it, not thinking it was real. The following week there was a ceremony on the beach and I was wearing a silly headdress. Everyone was standing around us and it all took place under a palm tree. When I got home and sobered up I thought I'd dreamt the whole thing. Shortly afterwards I came to my senses and left the hippie crowd I was with. I just walked out one morning and never came back. I went to stay with an aunt for a few months in St Albans and sorted my life out. I got a job, it was only as a shop assistant in a clothes shop but I started studying at night school and after a few other jobs I finally got a job in Manchester as a Personal Assistant to a large clothing company. That's where I met Sir Thomas, he was on the board and this was after his divorce of course, we started going out for meals and finally he proposed. I have been so happy and although he is older than me, you have to believe me it is the perfect marriage. Then it happened. Last year his eldest daughter got married, in Barbados. We went over for the wedding and going there brought it all back to me. I remembered the last time I was there and the wedding on the beach. My step-daughter was married on the beach and all the way through the ceremony I kept thinking, but this can't be legal can it? They are not in a church or any kind of building. Afterwards I said I wanted to go for a walk by myself, I went to the registry office in the town and asked to see the marriage records. When they turned up the page and I looked at the register I went cold. There on the page was my marriage, in black and white. Totally legal. My walk back to the hotel was very slow and laboured, I didn't know what to do. I had committed a crime. I was a bigamist. I was married twice. Then I thought Vic must have annulled the marriage or maybe he was dead. He certainly wasn't going to live long the way he consumed drugs. I had never heard of him since leaving London, I had started using my middle name Sara and had never been back to the any of my old haunts or kept in touch with any of the old crowd. All the way home on the plane I felt my stomach churning, not because of the flight but my unease of what a predicament I was in. When I got home I engaged a private detective to try and find Vic. I didn't tell him about the marriage I just wanted to know what had happened to him and where he was now. After a couple of weeks I had a report from the detective. Vic was still living in London, as a garage mechanic, he was living with a woman and they had two children, he was not married to her. When I read that report I felt sick. What was I to do? Tell Sir Thomas, ill as he was, it may push him over the edge, who could I confide in? If I said anything to his daughters they could easily turn against me for what I had done and the shame I would bring on the family. I would also of course be completely dis-inherited. It was then I heard your sermon about not being bound by our past." Lady Sara looked pleadingly at Charles. "You have to help me vicar, I don't know what to do or who to turn to."

Charles put his glass down and leant forward.

"Don't worry, I will do all I can, you have been very brave in telling me your story and I will have to think and pray about what the next steps should be. I will give it my full attention."

Lady Sara smiled. "I knew it would be right to come and talk to you, I feel it will be all right in the end and you will help me."

Charles felt he didn't deserve the confidence Lady Sara was placing in him, but he was the one she had confided in and now it was up to him to help her all he could.

Lady Sara left the vicarage in a better state than she had arrived.

Charles went out into the garden, to do some work but more pointedly to think and chew over the problems he was being asked to solve.

When Heather came back hot and sweaty, she put her gym bag down in the hall before going for a shower. She went into the study and one slight sniff was enough to tell her that Charles' visitor that afternoon was Lady Sara Hetherington. There was no-one else in the village that could afford or would wear that kind of expensive perfume. She went upstairs to shower.

Chapter Six

THE FOLLOWING week was quiet and it left the vicar time to think over what people had said to him. But then just as he thought the storm he had created had subsided there was another visitor.

There was a knock at the vicarage door, Heather went to the door and found Hazel Forrest standing there looking a little agitated. Hazel was a single women in her late forties, a country person, she lived in the large converted farmhouse on the edge of the village and ran the large successful market garden. She had lived in the village for over 20 years and was a passionate enthusiast for all things green. It was no surprise that she had cycled to the vicarage dressed in her green dungarees. Her face was flushed and her hair awry as she asked if she could see the vicar.

Heather showed her into the study asking if they wanted any refreshments, Hazel just asked for a glass of water which Heather brought and then went back to the kitchen to resume her baking pondering as she did so if this was another consequence of 'that sermon'.

Hazel sat in the big leather chair and looked intently at Charles, he tried to put her at ease, with little effect. Hazel looked agitated holding her hands together and twisting her fingers.

Charles smiled at her "Now, Hazel how can I help?"

"Well, Vicar as you know I don't come to church very often, more of a Harvest and Festivals person."

"You do an awful lot in the village Hazel, you are always there at the front in any community activity."

For the first time Hazel smiled. "That's the easy bit, that's what I like doing. It's when I stop and think and have time to myself, that's what I find difficult."

Charles frowned, wondering what was to come.

"It was your sermon vicar last Sunday, it really did hit me in a way I don't think a sermon has ever done before."

Charles groaned inwardly and thought to himself. That sermon certainly has a lot to answer for, the problems it has brought to the surface.

"I think that sermon seemed to resonate with quite a lot of people, I don't think I have ever preached a sermon with so much response. If you have something you want to tell me, I am here and can assure of complete confidentially."

Hazel took a deep breath and began to tell her story.

"You are the first person to know this story and it is one I am not proud of and I know I need to tell it to someone and see what can be done. I am not the person you think vicar, I have lived a lie for over 25 years and it has been on my conscience and I thought it would get easier, but it has not, it has got harder."

Charles tried to look reassuringly at her. "We all have secrets that we live with and they can also sometimes destroy us."

Hazel looked out of the window, looking beyond what was before her as if she was trying to look back in time.

"Here goes, it is not an easy story. My name is not Hazel Forrest it is Jean Gibbs, I was born in the North-East in Hexham. I was the only child in the family and I think my parents put a lot of store by me, what I would do, who I would marry, what I would accomplish in my life, things which they never did. It didn't work out like that. I loved the countryside, I liked farms and animals. I didn't like exams and school. That was their first disappointment. When I left school I got a job at a Market Gardeners, I was happy, my parents were not, they hoped that I would have gone to University and become I don't know what, perhaps a teacher!. In my teens I was quite a tomboy not interested in feminine things. I hated dresses and dances and all that. When I was 18 I realised I wasn't like other girls in Hexham, I didn't fancy boys, I was a Lesbian. I had a relationship with an older women in the village and my parents grew suspicious, when the found out, it resulted in an almighty row and me moving out of the house. They were involved in the local Abbey and feared that my behaviour would cause a scandal in the town. You have to remember this was the fifties and people were not as tolerant as they are today.

Charles smiled and wondered why humans were so besotted with sexuality and thinking that God would not approve of our actions, was he that interested?

I lived with the older women for a few years, then it broke up. I decided I wanted to do something else so I decided to go overseas. I volunteered for a Farming Programme in Africa and after a number of interviews went to Malawi to help a United Nations programme that set up small agricultural co-operatives. I loved it, the people, the job and at last I found that I was fulfilled. It was there where I met Hazel. She was the same age as me and we looked very similar, people always thought we were sisters. We fell in love and had a loving relationship, we worked together on various programmes for ten years. I came home briefly when my parents died to sort out things in Hexham and then return to Malawi. Hazel like me had a father who didn't approve of her sexuality and had even beaten her and thrown her out of the house. Her mother was more sympathetic and always kept in touch. He died and Hazel told me she was growing closer to her mother, like me she was an only child. I suppose we were like two peas in a pod sharing everything, our life, our work, our love. The life suited us both, we were outdoor women, free spirits and content with the simple things in life. We travelled and went on holidays together-not back to England but to other places in the world.

Then it all changed. She sipped from the glass of water.

Hazel received a letter from her mother, it was a different kind of letter, speaking as if she was telling her things she needed to know. She'd had a fall and was in a residential home for recouperation.

There was also another letter from the Matron to Hazel telling her that her mother was very ill, (although she didn't realise it herself) and if she wanted to see her again she should try to get home soon if she could.

Hazel was concerned and decided to go home for a few months to look after her mother. At that time we were working on a water project together, building a local dam and she prepared to leave. We parted and

I saw her onto the plane a small eight seater, as it took off with three other passengers on the way to the main airport in Lilongwe. That was the last time I saw Hazel alive. The plane crashed a few miles from the take-off strip. Its engine had seized and the pilot couldn't get it under control.

I heard an hour after she had gone that the plane had crashed with no survivors. It was as if someone had cut out my heart, I was bereft and walked around in a trance for days. We buried Hazel in the cemetery at the edge of the village by the dam which she had worked on and which would provide water for a number of villages. Then another letter arrived for her, this time from the Matron at the Residential Home saying her mother had deteriorated and would Hazel come quickly.

I decided to go back to England and go and see Hazel's mother, to tell her myself, the least I could do.

I packed up and went once more to the grave of Hazel and said my good-byes. I knew I would not be coming back.

I arrived in England and went straight to the Residential home not far from here in Littlehampton. It was then when something strange happened which I did not plan. The Matron met me and thought I was Hazel, I didn't have the chance to explain before she led me into the room and she had announced to the women lying in the bed, (who was obviously extremely ill), that her daughter had arrived. Hazel's mother smiled and I went over and held her hand. She was only half conscious and I just stayed with her, until she went finally off to sleep for the night.

The Matron was so pleased that her daughter had managed to get home to see her. I was tired and emotional from the journey and thought I would explain things later. The Matron gave me the handbag belonging to Hazel's mother, inside were a stack of letters, all from Hazel, obviously they had been read and re-read and treasured. There were also the keys to the house of Hazel's Mum, the place I am living in now.

I went there and very tentatively opened the front door and went in. It was an old person's house, tastefully furnished and everything in a very neat and tidy order. I went upstairs collapsed on the bed in the bedroom which obviously was Hazels, her things still in the room and pictures on the wall. It felt strangely comforting as if Hazel was still alive and with me. I was still grieving and this in a strange kind of way was helping me. I slept that night intending the following morning to begin to explain the confusion I had got myself into.

I woke feeling refreshed and went to the village shop to buy some milk and bread. I had only just walked in and from behind the counter the large red-faced lady shouted out to the shop full of customers. 'How nice to see you Hazel, how's your Mum going on, do send her our love.' Everyone turned to look at me and I managed a weak smile. I mumbled something and got the provisions and went out of the shop. This was getting more difficult, the longer I left it the harder it would become to tell everyone that Hazel was now dead. I suppose looking back I couldn't face up to saying that, I had hardly said it to myself. To allow people to believe in this deception seemed comforting, what harm was I doing?

I went to the Residential Home again in the afternoon determined to put things right and tell the truth. I was met by the Matron who immediately said how much ‘my mother’ had improved since my visit. She was still very ill but my visit had made her more contented, she felt she had finally been able to put things right in her family. The Matron thanked me for coming, I felt a huge fraud. Hazel’s mum was semi-conscious, I held her hand which seemed to re-assure her and I stayed with her for the afternoon. Before I left she opened her eyes, looked at me and smiled and said, look in the bureau in the front room 'I want you to put all my things in proper order.' She obviously had no reason to believe I wasn’t Hazel and in her condition accepted my deception.

I didn’t look in the bureau it felt like prying but I continued to go and see Hazel’s mum. I could see each day she was getting weaker and after four days she died. The Matron was very comforting and I found myself crying as she put her arms around me, I felt another link to Hazel had died and I was left bereft in the world.

That night when I returned to Hazel’s family home I went into the front room and sat down with a cup of tea at the bureau. I remember giving a huge sigh and opening the drawer. There were small piles of letters and bills all in order and arranged neatly. At the back there was a big manilla envelope with the words Last Will and Testament on them. I tentatively opened it up and read the contents.

The last will and Testament of Enid Forrest
I bequeath the house and all the contents to my

daughter Hazel. Also any monies I hold in bank accounts, stocks, shares, saving investments etc.
If my daughter is not alive at my death I bequeath my whole estate to my two cousins Gwendolyn and Mildred who now live in Seattle.U.S.A.
There were also some small bequests to various charities and local people.

I put the will back in the bureau and went out into the garden to think. Hazel had told me about the cousins. How awful they had made her childhood, how they used to bully her mother who could not see what kind of people they were. Both of them only lived for holidays and shopping. They had both married rich Americans and spent their time on cruises and shopping expeditions. Hazel had said that she had never met two more materialistic, vain and empty people in her life. They also disapproved of Hazel's sexuality and made no bones in telling everyone what they thought. These two would now inherit everything, this house, any funds in the bank, investments and spend it on themselves. I was so mad I walked round and round the garden thinking of how unfair it all was. Of how Hazel would have used the money for others and not on herself. I looked around the garden, quite large with two fields at the back which also belonged to the house and were rented out to a local farmer. The house itself was a large detached Georgian farmhouse with lovely views over the hills and the village. That night I opened a bottle of wine and consoled my sorrows.

During the night I woke up in a cold sweat, I got

up and went downstairs to make myself a cup of coffee. I sat curled up under a blanket on the settee and very slowly an idea began to emerge. Suppose I was to stay here and be Hazel? Everyone seems to think I am her and I had her passport and papers. She had no family in this country apart from her mother; her cousins had not seen her for years. People always commented how much alike we both looked. I could do the things Hazel would have done with the money. I could at least keep it out of the hands of the two cousins and Hazel would have approved of that."

Charles was amazed and incredulous although he tried not to show it. What a story and almost unbelievable but here was the proof sitting right here before him.

Hazel continued, it obviously helped her telling her story to someone else, it was like a dam bursting, the words just pouring out.

"The following morning I rang an undertaker and arranged the funeral. I decided to have it in the village and your predecessor Rev Dunford came to see me. He was a very nice man, he had never met Hazel, but her mother had told him all about her. He said he knew her favourite hymns and would handle everything. I tried to fill him in with little bits of information that Hazel had passed on to me but Rev. Dunford was so good and said he would take care of everything. The next few days were quite tense, I felt I was going to be found out as a fraud every moment. The hardest thing was registering the death. Sitting opposite a registrar pretending to be someone else and giving them details of Hazel's mother. The funeral also was something I was dreading. What happens if one of Hazel's old friends turn up? What about the cousins? What if there were other relatives who would be suspicious of me?

Then it happened. A phone call from the United States. The cousins were coming for the funeral. They would stay at a hotel in Littlehampton.

I went cold. I felt as if I was going to be revealed as a fraud and the whole word would collapse. I then went through the house and searched every drawer looking for things which may help me in my deception. I found scrapbooks and old letters. I poured over them taking in every detail. I even took an old photo of Hazel to the Hairdressers in Littlehampton and asked if I could have the same style. Hazel and I dressed the same and often exchanged clothes so that was no problem.

The cousins arrived and were just as awful as Hazel described, materialistic, selfish and self-obsessed, I don't think they would have noticed me if I had grown another head. They took little notice of me and obviously still disapproved of "Hazel". They visited the house and obviously were giving it the once-over looking at the furniture and ornaments to see if there were any antiques. They even made reference to the will asking if 'the old lady' as they called her had made one. I said I think so but we wouldn't be reading it till after the funeral.

I needn't have worried about the funeral. Rev Dunford did a great job and everyone seemed to be pleased to see me and spoke highly of Hazel's mother. A few people said how much I had changed-it must the African sun, but it seemed to go off alright.

The following morning was going to be another ordeal as the family solicitor was going to come and read the will at the house. The solicitor had met Hazel once after her father died but I needn't have worried, he was a very innocuous sort of man who didn't look too closely at people, he was far more interested in official papers.

We were all seated in the dining room, Rev Dunford and a few of Hazel's mother's old friends from the village and of course the two cousins who had been telling everyone of how inseparable they were from Hazel's mother and how they did all kinds of things together and cared deeply for each other.

After the formalities the solicitor read the will. I thought she would not have made another one but it was just like the one I had seen. Hazel was to get everything apart from some bequests to friends in the village and one for the church. When he came to the words 'if Hazel was not alive at time of my death then my whole estate would pass to my two cousins Gwendolyn and Mildred.' I looked at them when those words were read and if looks could kill they would have plunged a dagger into my heart at that very moment. Thankfully they left shortly afterwards obviously disappointed that they were to receive nothing until Hazel died. If only they knew I thought as I tidied up the house afterwards.

From then it was easy. I became Hazel. I knew her signature, the passport looked similar and there were no friends in England who would remember her that closely. I must say that these last 10 years I have tried to be Hazel in all things. It has helped in my grieving. I took back the fields and created a successful market garden which employs 20 people from the village. I try to put back into the community not take out and support everything which is going on here. I have had no other relationship since Hazel and am content living in her house, sleeping in her bed and doing things I believe she would do herself.

Charles looked at 'Hazel'..."That is an incredible story and almost unbelievable. You have certainly fooled everyone and there is no hint of suspicion in the village."

Hazel looked searchingly at Charles.

"What are you going to do vicar? Turn me in?"

"You have told me this in confidence and I aim to keep that confidence, however I would like to think it through and talk to you again".

Hazel smiled. "Thank you, I knew I was right, I could trust you, it has been such a relief to tell someone about it, I feel a lot easier in myself now."

She got up to leave and gave Charles a warm smile. She turned and gave him a hug.

Chapter Seven

HEATHER NOTICED that after a week there was a dramatic change in Charles. He seemed to have aged and there was something troubling him? She decided she must tackle it, even if it looked as if she was interfering.

"Charles, since that sermon I have noticed you have not been yourself. These visits in the last few weeks from members of the congregation have obviously upset you, is there anything I can do to help?"

He reached out over the table, taking her hand. "Thank you Heather for caring, there is nothing you can do, people have confided in me and I cannot betray their trust."

"But you can talk to me generally you don't have to be specific."

"Heather, this is a small community, I could give away something quite innocently and it would be seen as a betrayal. No, I have to solve this myself hopefully with a bit of help from the Almighty."

For the first time in their marriage Heather felt excluded. An outsider looking in, not able to help, not even knowing what the problems were.

Her eyes welled with tears but Charles did not notice.

"If you can't talk to me, then you must talk to someone! Why don't you go to the retreat centre for a few days and see Father Ambrose?"

With that she got up from the table and started

washing the dishes with her back to Charles so he couldn't see her tears.

Charles looked thoughtful. "Do you know that is a very good idea Heather! I am sure talking with someone like Ambrose can only help, he has known me for the last twenty years and I have always found his advice sound."

"I'm pleased that I have been helpful, why don't you stay a few days you need the rest, I am sure the parish can manage without you for a couple of days."

Charles got up from the table "Yes, I will go for a few days, I always enjoy my time at The Monastery, Rory can look after everything here. I will ring them now and see if they have any room."

With that he left the breakfast room, leaving Heather at the kitchen sink pleased that her suggestion had been taken up but still with the feeling of being excluded.

Two days later Charles set off for the Monastery, it was about a seventy mile drive, which he didn't mind as it was through some beautiful countryside and it helped settle his mind.

The Monastery always held a fascination for him. He had nearly become a monk himself but found he couldn't make the final commitments. He had over the years used the services of the monastery as both a retreat centre for personal development and also the wise spiritual counsel from Father Ambrose who had been his spiritual director for the last twenty years.

Charles arrived just before lunch. He felt very much at home as he drove up the long drive with the mature oak trees standing like sentries at the side of the road. It was set in its own grounds, a medieval monastery, which once must have housed as many as 200 monks. Now it was more like thirty and part of the accommodation had been converted into a retreat centre where individuals or groups could come. Those staying at the retreat centre could join in the services. There were six a day, each with their own particular theme and time. The ones Charles liked were the early morning one at 4-00am and also Compline at 7.30pm.

Charles had a simple lunch in the retreat centre and noted there were only a few clergy there sharing in a deanery retreat, he was thankful that he didn't know any of them so he could have some time to himself. There were also a few others, there for a private retreat.

After lunch he went to his room, he was intending to go for a walk but found himself lying on the bed reading a book and then going to sleep for a couple of hours. He woke to the sound of a large bell tolling for the afternoon service of Vespers. He went into the chapel admiring the high white sandstone arches and the tranquil air which always seemed to permeate the chapel. The monks voices echoing around the vast monastery, the last of the evening light coming through the lead lined windows and making pretty patterns on the chancel floor.

Charles found it all so peaceful. After the short service he managed to have a few words with Father Ambrose and they arranged to meet the following morning.

That night Charles sat up late making copious notes of the four cases. Getting the facts on paper always helped him. He wasn't sure if he would show them all to Ambrose but they would make good references for him and help make the questions he was asking clearer.

The following morning Father Ambrose greeted Charles like a long lost brother. Ambrose was tall, a spare figure whose robes hung loosely around his gaunt, slim form. A small white beard and his craggy features gave him an inquisitive air, but it was his eyes which drew you to him. They were a deep blue and looking at them gave a tranquil air, they seemed to be deep, they drew you in and you sensed a spirituality with him even if you knew nothing about him.

They began with prayer and Charles set about his story, telling Ambrose in detail about the sermon and the response from the congregation. He then went on to tell of his four visits calling them A.B.C.D. Although not disclosing the content of their stories, he said that each had something from the past they wanted to disclose. Each of the four could not hold this to themselves any longer and were looking to Charles to help them.

Ambrose interpreted. “Are we talking about criminal events?”

Charles hesitated. “Yes I think you could say that certainly in three of the situations and the fourth would have military implications through their court procedures.”

Ambrose looked thoughtful. “What about child abuse or a danger to others?”

“No, nothing like that and I don’t think any of them pose any danger to others, only to themselves.”

“Good, I am relieved about that. Things have changed in the world and in our world too. There are sins which we can no longer hold to ourselves even in the confessional."

"That is one of the questions I have for you. Are their stories to be regarded as confessions."

Ambrose clapped his large hands together and laughed.

"You Protestants, you do away with confession but you still believe in it and you still want to practice it. Did any of them see it as a formal confession?"

"No, they didn't although they wanted me to keep their confidences."

"Yes the dilemma, is it confession or not? You are aware that if it is a confession, after the absolution you can go no further with guidance or even referring to what has been said at any later date?"

"Yes, I do but that is what I am not sure of."

"How did they approach you?"

"Each one slightly differently, my sermon seemed to have opened up something from the past which they wanted someone to hear, they also wanted to know what to do now."

Ah! Ambrose clapped his hands again. "Here we have it. They came also for advice, then that is your answer, there was a confession of sorts but they also want answers to things that are troubling them."

"Are you seeing them again?"

"Yes, I said I would go away and think and pray about what they have said to me and see them next week."

"Can you give them answers?"

"Not at the moment."

Ambrose looked thoughtful. "I suppose the nature of what each has disclosed has an impact on their lives today."

"Yes with A it is guilt. B is an illegal arrangement which if uncovered would have deep repercussions for everyone close to that person. C is living a lie but if uncovered would probably have to go to prison. D has taken on another's identity. Indeed prison may be the result of all four."

Ambrose again looked thoughtful. "Let's deal with the problem of, is what they told you dealt with under the terms of confession. From what you have told me, I think I can give an answer.

You are not a Catholic Priest, and do not regularly take confessions in your church, they are not practising Catholics, they have had no formal teaching or practice of confession. They may call it confession but it cannot be confused with the sacrament of confession. If it had been confession it would have been about confessing and receiving absolution. There may be a penance, other things to do but it is not the same as asking for advice. No, what you have Charles in my opinion is confidential information not formal confession therefore you can act differently. You can give advice, after all that is one of the reasons why they have come to you. They also had a need to unburden themselves. I do not think though they should bind you, especially if we are talking about criminal acts."

Charles was pleased with the clarity of thought of Ambrose and relieved that he had come to share his burden.

"As to the advice, let me ponder and pray on that one, let us meet again tomorrow."

Charles thanked his friend for his wise counsel, already he was feeling better, he had someone to share this with and Ambrose was wise enough to deal with the problem without having to know all the details.

Charles enjoyed the rest of the day. He spent time in the monastic library and then walked around the grounds of the Abbey.

At Compline his thoughts went to Heather. Had he been fair to her? Had he excluded her? She was so much of a support to him in his ministry, in this though he had kept her at arms-length, she must have felt excluded. Was that the price to pay for being married to a priest, or was Charles being unfair and should he have talked more to her.

Questions and thoughts he had no real answer to.

Breakfast was always the same in the retreat house, boiled eggs and toast. There were copious in the quantity and amount. The eggs were always hard boiled but they were free range and the marmalade made in the monastery. Charles had no complaints.

Later that morning he met again with Father Ambrose.

"Did you sleep well Charles?"

"Yes I did, I slept both well and long and feel totally refreshed."

"Good I am pleased that the abbey here can be of some use to you clergy who are at the coal-face."

Charles smiled. He may be in a parish but Ambrose was exercising a very profound ministry here in the monastery and he knew that his advice and wise counsel were constantly sought after.

Father Ambrose came straight to the point. "I have given your problem much thought and prayer and come to some conclusions. As I said yesterday I do not think you should treat them as sacramental confessions. Each one I believed was looking for more, they came asking for advice. They were not practised in sacramental confession neither did they ask for it."

"Yes" said Charles "that is so, none of them asked for it, they just saw the initial confession as the end of it all."

"However" said Ambrose,"You are bound by confidentially, you cannot divulge what they have said to others, neither can you go the authorities. But there is something that can be done.

You can persuade them to put right what has been done wrong, you can encourage and counsel them to get their lives in proper order. You, I am sure, will stand by them whatever the consequences of their actions and the resulting solution."

"What if they refuse?"

Ambrose paused and looked out of the window. "Then it is going to be very difficult. You have to stand by the confidentiality, you cannot break that, you can only hope and pray they will see sense. We cannot use blackmail and say to people that they have to go to the authorities, we are not in the business of holding guns to people's heads."

Charles thought for a few moments. "In one of situations I have been compromised and if it comes out that I have known about this and done nothing about it, then I could be accused of covering it up and even aiding a criminal act. In another I received money, a large amount of money for the church believing that it came from a reputable source, the benefactor had not the right to give that money away."

Ambrose looked at his friend, his large piercing eyes going deep it felt into the very soul of his friend.

"Charles, you are a mature Christian and good

priest and pastor. I can only advise that you go with what your conscience allows you to do. God has guided you thus far, I am sure he is not going to desert you, that sermon was given for a reason and the final chapter of the story has not been written. These four people have come to you for a reason, they have been prompted to come, they realise that things are not right in their lives and they wish to put matters right. They have trusted you with something very precious, they will listen to you and I am sure accept what you have to tell them."

"Thank you Ambrose I feel I know what I must do, you have helped clarify my thoughts and see things in a new and different light. I now know what it is I have to do and say."

They prayed together and after breakfast the following morning Charles returned to the parish, much more at peace with himself.

Heather noticed a different Charles who had come back from the Monastery. He was confident and looked well, he did not have a tired expression and he even came back with some flowers and a box of chocolates. He must have realised he had excluded her she thought!

Chapter Eight

CHARLES WAS rather relived that Heather had decided to go out that morning! He was expecting a visitor and it wasn't going to be an easy conversation.

Lady Sara rang the doorbell and Charles thought for the first time he noticed age lines around the eyes as she came into the hall and entered the study.

After they were both seated Charles tried to put her at ease. "I'm glad you have come; I have thought and prayed long and hard over what you told me last week"

Sara looked up imploringly. "You are not going to tell anyone are you; you will keep my little secret?" Charles frowned.

"Sara, you have put me in a very difficult position, I conducted a marriage between you and Sir Thomas which was a sham, you were already married and you have committed bigamy."

Sara burst into tears and Charles wondered if he was being too harsh.

"I believe your story Sara that when you married in Barbados your lifestyle at the time was such that you had no commitment and saw everything as just another experience. I can believe that you took no store by it until you went to Barbados last year."

Sara dried her eyes. "Thank you for believing me."

"There is something I would like you to do."

Sara looked up imploringly.

"I want you to come clean with Sir Thomas. I want you to tell him the full story, he deserves your honesty."

"But you know how ill he is, the shock could kill him."

"That is a risk we will have to take. I think you underestimate him, he loves you and you will be able to come through this. If you tell him it will be for him to decide what can be done."

Lady Sara looked frightened. "But it means I risk everything, my marriage, my future, what about his two girls, they could turn against me?"

"If Sir Thomas dies, then I will have nothing, and be no-one."

"That is a risk you will have to take."

"And what if I do not agree to your suggestion?"

"Then I may have to inform the authorities that I believe I have conducted an illegal marriage and I now believe one of the parties was already married when I conducted the service and the partner is still alive."

Sara got up and coming towards Charles spat out the words. "You bastard!" With such venom that Charles was taken aback. Before he could react she stormed out of the study slamming the front door on her way out and leaving Charles to consider the wisdom of his actions.

Despite the reaction he knew he was right to tackle her and make her think. She had to realise that coming clean with Sir Thomas was the only way forward. They were man and wife, if their love was strong enough it could stand this, but even Charles knew it was a risk, it could go so horribly wrong and there was no certainty that Sir Thomas would stand by her, and what if the girls found out? With Sir Thomas very ill and likely to die soon it could have all kinds of legal ramifications.

Charles and Heather had a rather subdued and silent lunch. Heather had heard the door bang and guessed things had not gone well. She didn't want to ask him what had happened but noticed it had been quite a shock for him.

Later that evening the Colonel arrived.

He came straight to the point.

"Now vicar what's all this about? I came to you last week and expected my confidence would be respected, what are you intending to do?"

"I intend to do nothing it's for you to take any action."

The Colonel spluttered, "What do you mean?"

"Colonel, an injustice has been committed and you have chosen to live with it for over thirty years. That it came to the surface last week shows that you are still uncomfortable with it. I can understand the confusion of war but what I can't understand is you taking credit for something you haven't done and creating an image that at its best is false and what's more the actions of a coward."

The Colonel stood up and it looked as if he was going to strike the vicar. "My god sir, if you weren't a man of the cloth I'd strike you down for that, no-one has ever called me a coward."

"Perhaps they should have, for that's what you are. To take the credit for something you didn't do, to compound that by receiving a medal and living a lie, even to be responsible for the death of the man who was the hero. That for me is a pretty good definition of a coward. How would you justify your actions?"

The Colonel looked as if he would explode and then suddenly changed, his frame crumpled up and he drew back and collapsed into the chair.

"Yes, I suppose that's it. I'm finished, vicar, you have found me out. I have a revolver at home, you will have another funeral to take next week, and it will be mine."

Charles looked intently at the Colonel. "Somehow I don't think so. There is another way."

"I don't see how."

"I think you will agree an injustice has been done, I believe not intentionally by you but you let it continue. That injustice was done to the real hero, Pete Sanders. I want you to find his family, I will help you if you need me, I want you to give them your medals and say that an injustice has been done, he was the real hero."

"Vicar, you ask too much. I think my way is better."

"But then there is no justice."

"But I have my pride; it's the only thing I have left."

"I think it will take great courage to do what I ask. You could say it would be heroic."

"What do you know of heroism and warfare vicar? Preach your sermons, but don't tell me how to live my life."

With that he stormed out of the house, again the door hinges took the blast from his anger.

Charles had a very uneasy evening. Heather noticed how quiet he was during their evening meal but she didn't push things, she knew he must be dealing with very difficult matters. He was rather glad he had to go out to a meeting of the choir that evening, at least he could take his mind off the problems of others for a couple of hours.

The following afternoon Peter Frobisher arrived as arranged. He again looked nervous as he entered the vicarage and went into the study. He refused an offer of refreshments and went to sit down in the chair opposite the desk.

"I'm pleased to see you again, vicar I have felt a lot better since sharing my burden but I am not sure what I can do to sort out the situation. I am doing my best to give away funds and help worthy causes, I will of course continue to do this and if you have any suggestions I would be only too pleased to help."

"Yes, I can see your difficulty but I have come up with a few suggestions."

Peter leant forward in his chair keen to know what the vicar had to say.

"I think first of all you have to realise that the money you have had from the sale of shares from the Merryweather estate was not yours to use or give away. You have committed a criminal act no matter how you manage to massage it with generous gifts to various charitable causes."

Peter's mouth dropped open as Charles drew breath for he had not finished.

"After much thought and prayer I have come up with a way of keeping you out of the hands of the police or the Law Society. What I would like you to do is set up a separate trust with nominated trustees for the monies from the estate which are left. I would also think it is only right that you pay back any money you have spent on yourself or your family."

Peter took off his glasses and rubbed his eyes. “I can’t do this.........you don’t know what you are asking vicar.............I can’t find that amount to pay back...to this trust.......how would I explain it to my wife and family, my income would be vastly reduced.......I would be a broken man....”

Charles looked at him, he felt a little sympathy for a man who had made a huge mistake.

“This does not have to be done immediately, the money could be paid back to the Trust over a period of time.”

Peter now put on his glasses. “You ask too much vicar, I can’t do this, you will ruin me. I would lose all my respect, I cannot do what you ask.”

Charles looked at him with pity but also anger. “You have defrauded someone, you are a disgrace to your profession, you have spent money which was stolen and gone around giving money away which was not yours, playing the local benefactor.”

Peter stood up and came over to the vicar and pointed his finger at Charles.

“Let me remind you vicar that your church has benefited hugely from me and my generosity. Anyway, the matter is now finished, I thank you for time and advice, I wish I had never disclosed my problem to you in the first place but I would like to remind you, it was told to you in strict confidence and if you break that confidence I will make sure you never work as a priest again.”

With that he turned on his heels and went out of the study pausing only to pick up his hat from the hall before opening and then slamming the door behind him.

Charles sat in his study for a long time

contemplating what he had done, he had asked three people to do things which were against their nature to do. He had probably wrecked the church, with three leading members now all against him and probably wanting to get rid of him. Three families devastated by news which was unexpected and hard to assimilate. What had he done, and all because of one sermon.

It was not finished though. Later that afternoon there was another visitor. Hazel Forrest.

Again she was dressed in her working clothes and came in looking worried and pensive. When they had both gone in the study and sat down she quickly spoke out.

"I am not sure why you wanted me to come and see you. I have told you the full story, I didn't hold anything back."

Charles tried to look at her reassuringly. "I know you have been very honest but we cannot just leave it there, something must be done, you are living a lie."

Hazel stood up and looked at the vicar reproachfully. "You mean you want me to tell the truth. Let those two money-grabbing cousins have the farm and Hazel's money. Let them spend it on themselves to go on some more luxurious cruises and buy more things to pander to their greed. They would close the farm down as soon as they had their hands on it and sell it for houses, how would you explain that to the 20 parishioners who would be thrown out of work."

Charles looked forlorn and without an answer. "We have to come up with something which will help you tell the truth and stop living a lie."

Hazel came closer to Charles. "I will not let Hazel's memory be destroyed by those two greedy cousins. I know what I have done has not been right but I believe I have respected Hazel's memory and done something she would have wanted had she lived. I have not done it for myself I have done it for her and the village."

"I respect what you have done, you have done it for others but there are things which are not right, you cannot go on pretending to be someone who has died, living their life."

Hazel looked intently at the vicar. "You have to understand I will not let those thieving cousins get their hands on the farm or Hazel's money. I will do anything to stop that. So please don't threaten me with exposure. If you do, you will not realise what trouble you have brought down upon your head."

With that she left the room, leaving the door to the study open and Charles staring after her. She let herself out of the vicarage; surprisingly she didn't slam the door.

Charles sat in the study wondering indeed what he had brought upon himself.

Later on Heather came in carrying a tray with two glasses of gin and tonic on it. "I think you may need this; it's been a long day."

Charles smiled, it had and had not gone as well as he hoped.

He took a large sip and smiled at Heather. "I think I have wrecked the lives of four leading families in this community."

Heather looked puzzled.

"You may as well know this. They each told me things after that sermon I preached. They were things which were buried in the past but needed resolving. They may not admit it but the past was putting a hold on them which they dare not admit to. I could also destroy them".

"The Colonel, Lady Sara, Hazel Forrest and Peter Frobisher! You could not pick four more leading members of the church or the community if you'd tried." Heather looked at Charles sympathetically. "Shall I start packing? Somehow I think we may not be welcome here for much longer."

Charles smiled. "You may be right, but my conscience is clear. I have never felt more assured than I do now."

Heather came over and gave him a kiss and cuddled up to him.

"That's why I am so proud of you. Stick to your principles, that's what I admire you for and that's why I married you."

They kissed again, content in each other's arms, little realising that these were some of their last moments together.

There were others in Little Stanbury who were not as comfortable, who were only thinking of past indiscretions and how now they were coming back into their lives to taunt and to haunt them and for each of them the future looked very bleak indeed. Had they made a mistake in confessing, how could the genie be put back in the bottle, what could be done, what action could they take?

Chapter Nine

A FEW DAYS after Charles death, people started calling at the vicarage. The Bishop came to give what support he could, to say of course how regrettable this accident was as Charles was such a good priest. The Bishop would preside over the funeral service and would liaise with Charles' curate about the details. Heather thought the Bishop was a bit patronising, especially when he raised the question of allowing Heather to stay at the vicarage for as long as she wanted, until she had alternative accommodation sorted out. Heather hadn't realised this, but it seemed so obvious, Charles' death meant that she would have to vacate the vicarage, where would she go? What would she do? She was only in her late forties; she suddenly had to start planning a new life, now at this time.

Rory, Charles' curate, she found more helpful. She told him her fears and how useless she felt the Bishop had been, he raised his eyebrows and said more in a glance than in a long sentence.

She felt Rory was someone she could open up to, her sister Joyce was well-meaning, but too fussy, she was different to Heather, always bothered about the practicalities of life, Martha to Heather's Mary. Heather was rather relived when Joyce asked would she mind if she went back to her family for a few days and she would return for the funeral. Heather was inwardly delighted, she wanted time on her own, time to gather her thoughts, time to work out what had happened, time to let the shock of the last few days 'sink in'.

After Joyce had gone, she invited Rory over for a simple tea. She wanted to talk to him about the funeral, making him tea would make her eat and it helped if she kept herself busy.

They sat down to a simple meal of ham, egg and chips, it had been one of Charles's favourites and Heather just wanted to go on familiar lines that she knew.

They had just finished tea when the doorbell rang and a rather bedraggled figure of Lady Sara was standing at the door holding a large bunch of flowers. It had been raining and she had walked from the Hall. "O do come in Lady Sara please, Rory is here but you don't mind him do you."

"No, not at all, he may be able to help with my quandary."

"Quandary, what do you mean?"

Sara tried to look casual. "Oh, something and nothing, I really came to see how you are and if there is anything we can help with."

"Thank you for your concern, and these flowers are lovely, it was so thoughtful of you."

"Sir Thomas as you know is not very well but he sends his best wishes and would like to help if there is anything we can do. He wondered if you would allow us to organise the catering for you after the funeral. We know a few caterers and would be more than happy to do this for you. Charles was such a good vicar and will be such a great loss to the church and the community."

"Thank you." said Heather. "That will be such a great help, when I have thought more about the organisation I will let you know."

"No trouble, we will be only too willing to help." Lady Sara was obviously looking uncomfortable about raising the next question, but it was something she had to ask.

"I hope you don't mind my troubling you about something. At a time like this, it seems so selfish," Lady Sara did look concerned.

Heather tried to put her at her ease."No, go on, if I can help I will, and I am sure Rory will to."

Rory nodded.

Lady Sara was having difficulty finding the right words to say.

"You see, I came to see your husband last week, about a close friend. It was about her marriage and there were some questions about the legality of an early foreign marriage. Charles said he would check and come back to me, I was hoping for an answer and wondered if he had left any papers or anything about it. I talked to him in confidence of course but I thought if he had written anything down, it may be useful to my friend. I really am sorry to bother you at a time like this but it is so important to my friend."

Heather looked puzzled. "Lady Sara I can confirm that anything you said to my husband remains confidential. No, he didn't tell me anything nor as far as I know write anything down. I will check though and let you know."

Rory tried to interject helpfully. "If I can be of any help, I am trained in marriage preparation and also we have to go through all the legalities of being our own registrar. I know a little of marriages in other counties. Was it in Europe?"

Lady Sara realised she had gone too far and desperately wanted to retract her question and just get out of the vicarage.

"Thank you, I shouldn't have asked at a time like this. Forget it. Yes, please forget all about what I have asked, my friend will now have to do her own research."

With that she made her apologies and left.

After seeing her out Heather came back into the room and sat down. She looked quizzically at Rory.

"Well, what did you make of that?"

Rory smiled. "The old one, I have a friend who has a problem"...... I've had quite a few of those, I'm really surprised people still use them, they are so easy to see through."

Heather looked thoughtful. "She must be pretty desperate to come round to a grieving widow and ask that kind of question, I wonder what she did consult Charles about?"

After thinking for a few moments a thought came to her mind. "Charles was very good at keeping confidences. I knew something was troubling him; it was after that sermon he preached. The following week four people made arrangements to see him, usually when I was out. Charles was very troubled by what they said to him and it even made him take a few days at the retreat centre to think things through. When he came back he seemed to know what to do, although he told me nothing. He said he would have to speak to the four people again. Wait a minute, yes, he did tell me something, he said each had told him about something in their past which if it was disclosed would have serious consequences for themselves, their families, the church and the community."

Rory gave a low whistle and exclaimed. “Wow, this is heavy stuff and what a motive!”

Heather looked startled. “Motive, what do you mean Rory? You don’t mean Charles could have been murdered?”

Rory immediately regretted what he had said. “No, you misunderstand me, it’s heavy pastoral material and it is so sad that Charles died while he was in the middle of sorting it all out.”

He desperately tried to change tack.

“He didn’t leave any private or confidential papers did he?”

“No, I don’t think so, I haven’t checked his study, he spent a long time in there over the last few days and he could have written some notes. The Bishop said he would deal with anything confidential in his papers.”

They both laughed at once, the thought striking each of them at the same time that the Bishop was the last person Charles would want dealing with any personal or confidential issues.

As Rory walked home, his mind was troubled. He was angry with himself for being so foolish as to plant the vague notion in Heather’s mind that there could be motives which could mean instead of an accident it was murder you were looking at.

Yet, he himself couldn’t work out the accident. Charles was a fit strong man; you don’t just fall and hit your head and then stumble back to your chair. The bumbling policemen who came and investigated looked as if he would take any answer as long as it didn’t mean him getting involved in a lot of paperwork. He was known for his thirst for beer and the frequency of his visits to the Red Lion and not renowned for detective skills.

After Rory had gone, Heather went into Charles study and for the first time since he had died, went and sat at his desk. Not the tidiest of people, yet there was some order in the different piles of files and books on the desk. Worship material, a pile of parish correspondence, another on the Parochial Church Council. She looked in the drawers. The top ones contained pens and rubber bands, stationery and other bits and pieces. The lower ones files on their bank accounts, other personal files on holidays and insurance. She dreaded having to start and go through them all, something which she would have to face in the days ahead.

And then right at the bottom a newish file with just two words on it. That Sermon written on it. She opened it and found another word this time written in red felt tip marker pen. CONFIDENTIAL.

She put the file down and left the study. She went into the kitchen and started clearing the table and doing the washing up. It always helped her to think. What was she to do? Should she read the file? Should she hand it over to the Bishop? Should she destroy it without looking at it? Should she give it to Rory and let him deal with it? There was another question she wanted answering, what would Charles have her do?

That to her was the most important one to answer and when the washing up and tidying the kitchen was complete she knew the answer.

She poured herself a large gin and tonic, went into the study, sat down at the desk and opened the file.

What she read amazed her. They were Charles' notes on what four people had confided to him. She was uneasy reading them, it seemed like prying, but some sense had to be made of the events of the last two weeks or these questions would live with her for the rest of her life. At first there was shock and disbelief that four such upstanding people of the village had such secrets. Secrets, which they had lived with for so long, being careful to hide and conceal but yet if disclosed to others could bring each person crashing down. She was proud that Charles' sermon seemed to have been the catalyst for each person's disclosure and confession. She could see how Charles was handling it in a very logical and caring way, not just following the rules but seeking justice and following for him what was the right path. She felt so proud of him and wished he was there for her to give him a hug.

She was intrigued by what Charles had asked each person to do. There must have been a feeling that confession was enough and it would go no further. You could get something off your chest and no-one would think any more about it.

Each of the four seemed to react in a very similar way to the tasks Charles had written down, saying it would demand a lot from each person, not least humility and that things would never be the same again.

She closed the file and put it away carefully. Now, a new question was uppermost in her thoughts. What must she do now? She also remembered a word Rory had used and then tried to retract it. Motive! What she had read made her feel that these four people each had a different motive to see Charles dead. A cold shiver ran down her spine and for the first time since Charles' death she felt very much alone and frightened.

That night was a long one and a difficult one for Heather. She felt she hardly slept, having to account in her mind for every tiny creak and noise in the house, when she finally dozed off the dawn was already breaking.

It was the phone that woke her up. It was the Colonel; a slight shiver ran down her spine remembering her husband's notes. He wanted to come and see her, would this morning be suitable? She hesitated but realised that she had no option. He was the vicar's warden for goodness sake. Yes, she said, could he come around 11'o'clock? After she put the phone down she rang Rory.

"Can you come round around 10 o'clock, I need you to see something."

She made some strong coffee and had it ready for Rory when he came in.

"Rory, I want your help, I cannot do this alone and I know Charles thought very highly of you and trusted you, I do too."

Rory smiled. "Of course I will do anything I can to help you, what is it you want?"

Heather took a gulp of the strong coffee.

"Last night after you left I looked in Charles' study and found a confidential file. I wasn't sure what to do with it, should I destroy it before reading it, just hand it over, but then I thought, what would Charles want me to do? That seemed to help me and I knew in such circumstances Charles would want me to read it."

Rory smiled at her. "I think you made the right choice."

"I now think you should read it." With that she tossed the yellow file marked confidential over to Rory.

Rory looked up. "You really think I should?"

Heather looked at him. "After I read it, I realised I may be in some danger, I can't confide in anyone else, Charles trusted you and I do too. I need your help."

Rory looked apprehensive wondering if his worst fears were being realised. He picked up the file and started reading.

When he finished he closed it and took another gulp of coffee.

"Wow" was his reaction. "What a mess."

"Yes" said Heather who hadn't taken her eyes off him the whole time he was reading the file. "And what's more, suspect number two arrives to see me in half-an-hour, the Colonel."

Rory looked up. "You mean you believe each of these had a motive to kill Charles?"

"I do." said Heather confidently. "I have been thinking of nothing else all night and after he has gone we are going to do some detective work of our own."

"Am I Dr. Watson to your Sherlock then?" They both laughed.

"Well at least you didn't call me Miss Marple?" Heather said smiling.

At eleven o'clock prompt there was a loud knock at the door.

Heather ushered the Colonel into the lounge and he looked quizzically at Rory before turning to Heather?

"I'm sorry, I thought you would be on your own."

Heather motioned for them both to sit down. "You can talk freely in front of Rory, he is helping me sort out the funeral and also Charles' affairs. Charles has left his study in such a mess and I don't know where anything is. Rory is being a great help."

The Colonel coughed uneasily," Yes well, as vicar's warden I was going to offer my help."

Heather spoke confidently.

"You needn't trouble yourself, we have everything in hand."

The Colonel moved uneasily in his seat, "Is there anything I can do about helping arrange the funeral?"

Heather smiled at him. "Thank you for offering, and yes there will be a lot of arrangements to make once we know the date, the undertaker is coming round this afternoon. I can be in touch then if you like and you can be the link with the church."

"Yes of course, the least I can do, damn good fellow your husband, such a loss. Have they said anything more about the accident?"

Heather looked pensive. "They just say it was a terrible accident, the police seem satisfied that Charles hit his head on the garden steps. It was so sudden."

"Yes......yes....a shock for us all." You could see that the Colonel was uneasy with any expression of emotion and soon got up to leave. Just as he about to leave he turned to Heather.

"There was just one thing I need to ask?"

"Yes." Heather looked quizzical.

"The Bishop has asked me to take care of any confidential papers you understand." Again he made a nervous cough. "I don't suppose you have come across any?"

Heather frowned. "You mean Church minutes and the like, there are plenty of those."

"No." again she wasn't helping him and he was very uneasy. "No, these would be confidential papers, perhaps notes he made about confidential matters regarding parishioners. We wouldn't want them falling into the wrong hands would we?" He made a nervous laugh.

Heather frowned; "No, I haven't found anything like that. Charles was so good at keeping confidences he never talked to me about pastoral issues and what people talked to him about."

"No, of course not, if you want I can go through his papers in the study."

Heather moved in front of the study door. "Perhaps after the funeral, let's get that sorted first."

"Yes, yes of course, thank you Heather I will be in touch, if there is anything I can do just let me know."

When he had left Heather and Rory returned to the kitchen.

Heather put the kettle on. "Well, Rory what do you make of that?"

Rory looked out of the window into the garden. "I'd say he was a worried man. That bit about the Bishop asking him to look after any confidential papers is a load of rubbish; I've never known him ask a church-warden to do that sort of thing. No, our Colonel is a worried man and if you were putting it in military terms you would say he was surrounded on all sides and doesn't know which way to turn."

Heather sat down at the kitchen table.

"Did you believe that note Charles wrote about him? About him being a coward. Taking another man's glory and medal, not to mention, accidentally shooting him in the back!"

"That's serious stuff and would make a man panic, if he thought it would come out."

"By the way, you were right about Lady Sara! It wasn't a friend she was asking about it was herself. My God a bigamist! That would set the tongues wagging in the village."

"Not to mention the inheritance and what happens should anything happen to Sir Thomas." added Rory.

Heather looked at Rory with an imploring look. "Rory, I want to ask you a big favour, will you stay here while all this is going on. I don't think I could bear to be alone, at least at night. I can make up the bed in the spare room. You don't need to be here all day just at night when it gets dark, it's a very big house."

Rory reached out and held her hand. "Of course I will, don't worry, and I will be discreet, I will park my motorbike around the back. We wouldn't want the neighbours talking would we?"

They both laughed.

Heather joked. "If they knew what we know, I think Mrs Oaks at the village post office wouldn't get any work done for weeks. Can you stay for lunch and then I need your help in the garden."

Rory liked Heather; she was different to most clergy wives. She had an openness and a love of life which wasn't narrowed by Christianity but rather fulfilled by it and she seemed to embrace the world rather than shrink from it.

After lunch they both went out into the garden. "Now Rory, this is going to be very difficult for me! But you have to promise that we keep going, even if I get upset." Rory was beginning to get an inkling of what they were going to do.

The chair that Charles had sat on that fateful day was still there, it was in a different position and Heather moved it into the position she remembered it to be in. She then went into the garage and brought out an old straw Panama hat which had belonged to Charles.

"Now you sit here with the hat on and read a book." She gave him a book she had brought out of the house.

"Right, what can you see?"

"The bottom end of the garden."

"You can't see the gate can you and anyone coming into the garden by the side passage?"

"No, just the garden."

"Right, now where would you have to fall to hit your head?"

Rory got up and went forward two paces; he then went forward another pace and said, "It would have to be on that top step."

"Right." said Heather, "Fall down and let's see how it looks."

He lay on the floor with his head on the top step; it was not an easy position to lie in.

Heather then spoke. "If I remember correctly the head wound was at the side, can I paint this marker pen on your head?" Rory smiled as she took a red lipstick out of her purse. She put a red mark on the side of his head.

"Now lay down with that red mark against the step."

Try as he might Rory couldn't do it in a natural position at all.

Heather watched noting everything down on a pad of paper.

Rory had to give up. “I can’t do it. I would have to twist my body round in such a difficult way, I would have to be a contortionist.”

“Exactly.” said Heather triumphantly. “That’s what P.C. Plod missed. He didn’t realise Charles could not have fallen against the steps and hit his head. Now, stagger back to the chair.”

Rory went backwards towards the chair and slumped into it.

“The hat!” exclaimed Heather “We’ve forgotten the hat!”

“Why would someone who has just fallen and hurt themselves, want to put on a hat?" exclaimed Rory.

“Exactly, another one missed by PC.Plod. Now, let’s look at what happened when I came into the garden.”

She went into the kitchen returning with a tray of plastic cups and a plastic jug.

“I came out and saw Charles sitting in the chair. I reached this point,” and she drew near the table, “ I then saw the trickle of blood.” She put the tray down and went over to Rory and drew on his face again, this time a red line. “I hope you don’t mind all this?”

Rory smiled reassuringly, “Not at all, if this helps in bringing Charles’s killer to justice, then it’s a small price to pay.”

Heather went back to pick up the tray and told Rory to act as if he was asleep.

She then came down the garden path and suddenly shrieked dropping the tray and running over to Rory.

“I came over, took off his hat and saw the blood. I must have screamed and the neighbours came running. After that it was all a blur.”

Heather picked up the cups and they both sat at the table.

"Have we proved that Charles could not have fallen on the ground, hit his head on the step and then returned to his chair and put his hat on?"

"I think so." said Rory.

"Wait a minute, I remember PC.Plod asking me if Charles had been drinking. He must have thought Charles had been drinking and had too much, he must have thought he was drunk."

"As our policeman spends so much time in the Red Lion, perhaps he thinks all crimes relate to alcohol!"

"I think you may be right."

They went indoors to await the funeral director and there was a message on the answer machine in the study. It was from Peter Frobisher asking if he could call and see Heather. They both looked at each other and smiled.

Rory remarked wryly. "As Sherlock would say, the game is afoot"

"It is indeed." replied Heather.

They were both there when the undertaker came. A rather supercilious man, specialising as he thought, in understanding and sympathy, which came over as trite and insipid condescension. Heather asked for the funeral to take place in ten day's time, she didn't want it to be rushed as people would be coming from different parts of England. She chose a simple coffin, against the wishes of the undertaker who was hoping for something a little more prestigious for such a large service. The church would do the flowers and the reception would be at the Parish Hall.

The undertaker seemed to be underwhelmed with the arrangements, but nevertheless accepted them and left.

Heather then rang Peter Frobisher asking him to come round at 7pm.

"You do see why I need you here Rory I couldn't face him by myself."

"Of course, I will be here, besides, I enjoy your cooking".

They both laughed.

At 7 o'clock there was a rather nervous knock at the door. Heather ushered Peter Frobisher into the lounge and again, he was surprised to meet there the curate Rory Coverdale. He looked at Heather.

"I thought we would be alone?"

Heather tried to put him at ease. "Rory is helping sorting out the funeral arrangements and he has been a great help," as she winked at Rory.

"Do sit down Peter, would you like a drink?"

"Normally I wouldn't but if you have a small gin and tonic?"

Heather poured out three large gin and tonics.

"Here you are Peter. Now how can we help you?"

Peter was taken aback; he was here to help Heather.

"Well, I came to express my condolences. Charles has been very helpful to me, and I always found his services very challenging and thoughtful."

Heather glanced at Rory.

"Thank you, that is very helpful at a time like this."

Peter took a large gulp of the gin & tonic "I was wondering?"

Heather leaned forward. "Yes?"

Rory smiled inwardly and thought that women are very shrewd.

"I was........was...wondering if I could be of any help with the confidential papers.

As a solicitor of course I am used to dealing with such matters. I wondered if you needed a hand in going through the paperwork."

Heather smiled. "Thank you Peter, that is such a kind offer, I may take you up on it later, the Bishop has also offered to do this and so has the Colonel." They both saw Peter visibly wince.

Peter was not beaten. "I would offer of course my professional services for free." After a little hesitation he added. "Did Charles leave any confidential papers?"

Heather gave the slightest of glances to Rory which Peter noticed.

"No, I don't think there was anything special." She quickly went on. "He left a Will which will be straight forward, we don't have any children, and there is no property."

Peter made some general comments about Heather now having to look after her own interests now and he hoped the church would make adequate provision for her future. Shortly afterwards he gave his apologies and left.

Heather and Rory sat in the lounge over a cup of coffee talking.

"What now Watson?" she asked looking enquiringly at Rory.

"Well." said Rory "In the detective novels a trap is set or someone will make a move?"

Heather looked pensive; "Do you think that will happen?"

"It is something that we should consider, if someone has already committed murder, surely they would want to protect themselves."

A shiver went down Heathers spine,

"I'm glad you're here Rory! I don't know how I would have coped without you."

The phone rang. Heather picked it up, it was Hazel Forrest.

After she had spoken for a few minutes she rang off and Heather came and sat down looking thoughtful.

Rory said. "What did she have to say?"

Heather looked across the room at him, "How she wanted to express her condolences and ask if she could do anything for me, she said she was going to call round in the morning. She also said something rather strange. She asked if Charles had been in touch with anyone in America?"

Rory smiled; "I think we should be extra vigilant tonight in locking up the house."

They both agreed.

Chapter Ten

RORY AWOKE with the sun streaming through the bedroom window and Heather knocking loudly on the door. "Rory, you have to come downstairs quickly, something awful has happened."

He shot out of bed and quickly put on some clothes before sprinting downstairs.

He found Heather at the door of the study. She was looking at the papers strewn around the floor, the curtain flapping at the broken window, the whole room in a mess.

Rory put a consoling arm around her. "I can't believe we didn't hear anything." Then he said in panic. "The papers, Charles papers, were they in there?"

Heather smiled. "No I put them somewhere safe, they are in my bedroom in my underwear drawer."

Rory blushed slightly.

"What a relief that is. I suppose we should call the police. Let's see what they say this time."

About twenty minutes later PC. Burns arrived this time accompanied by a plain clothes officer.

After examining the study they went into the kitchen and Heather made them all cups of coffee.

PC Burns asked if anything valuable had been stolen. Heather said she didn't know but nothing of great value was kept in the study, there were mainly church papers. She would check later and give the police station a full description.

PC. Burns said he had a theory. Rory felt he

wanted to crown him but refrained because of Heather. He puffed out his large chest.

"In my long experience of being in the force this was all too common. A death, then sadly someone sees the chance of a burglary, they think there will be no-one in the property, it gives them a free hand. Also, very sadly the bereaved may not know what has been stolen."

Rory felt he had to say something. "But why didn't they go through the rest of the house?"

"Probably heard a noise and panicked, who knows?"

Heather asked. "What about fingerprints?"

The plain clothes man spoke. "They used gloves. Looks like a professional job. We have seen others like this, I am afraid they do target recently bereaved families."

They gave Heather an incident number for the insurance and also helpfully a number of someone who would fix the window quickly.

After some general advice which Heather and Rory thought pretty useless they both bade their farewells saying they would keep a special watch on the house in the next few days. Just in case the burglar came back.

Heather felt a shiver down her spine and collapsed in tears in the arms of Rory after they had left.

"Are we out of our depth Rory? Should we have told them our suspicions?"

"How could we? It would be breaking the confidences of four people. Can you imagine PC Burns keeping all that information to himself after a few pints down at the Red Lion? No, hard as it is we have done the right thing and we must continue."

Heather agreed and gave Rory's hand a reassuring squeeze.

"Yes, you are right. I have to be strong because of seeking justice for Charles. Let's clear up the study."

They both set about cleaning up the broken glass and putting the papers and books back in some sort of order. They were just about finished when the doorbell rang. It was a very agitated Lady Sara...

"I am so sorry to hear about the burglary last night, was anything taken?"

Heather didn't say that Rory was staying with her, just that nothing of value was taken, and they had only been in the study.

Lady Sara said hesitatingly, "I suppose that's where Charles kept his confidential papers?"

Rory came in. "We are pretty sure that nothing was taken, they seem to have been disturbed."

Lady Sara looked relieved. "If there is anything I can do. If you would like to come and stay at the Hall for a few days Heather?"

Heather politely declined the offer saying she would be alright as her sister was coming.

As expected Lady Sara's visit was followed by others, predicable in their concern and questions and probing as to what exactly had been stolen. The Colonel almost insisted on moving in to protect Heather and she had to say a white lie that her sister was coming to stay later that evening. Peter was his usual nervous self and looked a very worried man. Then Hazel Forrest arrived. Rory made her a cup of coffee as she talked to Heather. Hazel was a real countrywoman, dressed in her green overalls, her hair awry, with a strong tanned weather beaten face. She was concerned about the break-in but it was also the first time she had seen Heather since Charles' death.

When she had gone Rory and Heather sat in the kitchen. Heather confirmed that Hazel too had asked about anything been stolen from the vicarage study. She did ask something curious said Heather. She asked if Charles made notes of meeting he had with people. She also asked again if he had contacted America?

"What did you say?" asked Rory.

"I said I wasn't sure."

"Good answer," said Rory. "She was obviously worried about the cousins and if Charles had contacted them."

After they had finished tidying up the study Heather made them both some coffee and they sat down to take stock of the situation.

"Well," began Rory. "It seems we are on the right lines, our suspicions are justified."

"Yes." said Heather "But which one is the murderer? They can't all have done it, but one of them has."

"Each has a good motive for not agreeing to Charles' requests to them. They all would be more than embarrassed if the truth was known about them. Their lives would be changed completely, it may even mean prison for some of them."

Heather shivered. "One of them sat here today and tried to console me, yet they killed my husband and also burgled my property. How could they do such a thing?"

Rory and Heather sat in silence for a few minutes pondering on their next move.

Heather broke the silence. “What would Sherlock do, Watson?”

Rory looked up, “He would set a trap.”

“Exactly,” said Heather, “And that’s what we must do.”

“It could be dangerous.”

“I am sure we are more than a match for any of our adversaries.”

Rory was not as sure but kept silence. One of the four was a murderer and would they be prepared to murder again to protect their deceptions? He felt they would and he and Heather were playing a very dangerous game. But what was the alternative? The local police were out of their depth and were more than useless. Disclosing the confidential papers of Charles’ would be very dangerous and Rory was not sure how it would be viewed by the church, a priest’s notes on confidences even confessions handed over to the police.

Could they really just let things lie? The burglary had proved they could not sit back and do nothing. Perhaps Heather was right, attack was the best form of defence.

Heather made some sandwiches to go with the homemade soup. As they sat down for lunch they starting setting the trap.

“How are we going to do this Rory?”

Rory paused from eating the soup. “I‘m not sure, it seems the most difficult and dangerous part will be to separate the murderer from the others.”

“Yes” said Heather, “Is the burglar the same person as the murderer?"

Rory looked thoughtful. “I’m not sure, but probably it is someone who would do something like that to protect themselves.”

"Does that rule out Hazel who only came this morning after the burglary?"

Rory pondered for a few moments. "No I don't think so, she could have done the burglary and came back to make us think it couldn't be her. The burglar also never found what they came for, they were guessing that Charles kept some kind of notes of the meetings."

Heather thought for a moment and then came up with an idea. "We could say that we found some confidential papers and we are going to give them to the Bishop."

"But that would mean all four of them turning up. Somehow we have to find a way of confronting them separately in a way which reveals their true motives."

Lunch continued with them both deep in thought.

"This is not as easy as I thought it would be?" said Rory looking for inspiration.

Heather cleared the table. "Look, let's go through everything again and set it out on paper, some plan may occur to us."

"Good idea Sherlock, do you need to fetch your pipe."

Heather smiled and ruffled his hair. She liked Rory being around and she certainly needed him at the moment. Rory found a pad of paper and started writing.

"Let's go through each of our suspects, which one had the most to lose. Who had the best motive for murder?"

A shiver went down Heathers back. This was her husband they were talking about not just a game of Cluedo. But she realised, it must be done.

"Let's start with her Ladyship."

"She certainly has a lot to lose."

"If her marriage to Sir Thomas is proved to be bogus, she would lose her title."

"His children could turn against her."

"Sir Thomas could turn against her as well."

"The police would want to investigate a bigamous marriage."

"I did some research and she could expect a few months in prison if found guilty."

"Then there is the shame in the village."

"Loss of money and status."

"Not to mention Sir Thomas, it could be fatal for him if all this came out. He's not young, it could devastate him."

"Let's give her 9 out 10 for motive." said Rory.

"Agreed."

Rory considered. "Next, Peter Frobisher."

"He would lose his fortune."

"He would no longer be able to play the local benefactor."

"His family would be devastated."

"The Law Society and the Police would have to be involved."

"It could result in a prison sentence."

"He may have to repay the money."

"His status in the village as the local benefactor would be finished."

"His family may turn against him for the shame he has brought to them."

"He is another 9 out 10."

"Let's see if the Colonel is any different." Rory said.

"His status is what he prides the most."

"He would be finished. Not just a liar but also a coward."

"He could have put things right but chose not to."

"He has a gun."

"By his own admission he has killed before."

"Pride can be a terrible thing and people can think if they lose it they cannot live."

"He threatened something like that according to Charles' notes."

"His whole life revolves around his status."

"I would give him 10." said Heather.

"Not sure ...I think him a nine."

Rory went on "Now what about Hazel or should I say Jean Gibbs. Living a lie and impersonating another person is a criminal offence."

"You could argue she has taken the Farm and money which was not hers."

"She has defrauded the cousins in America no matter how awful they are!"

"She has done good for the village but will the villagers see it that way when they know the truth."

"She said she would do anything to protect Hazel's memory and stop the money going to the cousins."

"Another 9 out of 10."

Heather looked puzzled. "Is this helping? I can't see we are any farther forward?"

Rory looked at the scribbles on the piece of paper.

"Let's continue something may strike us. Let's now look at what Charles asked each one of them to do and judge how hard it would be for each one of them to do it . Have you Charles' papers?"

"Yes they are upstairs...in my..."

"Your underwear drawer! If I become a burglar I would know where to look in a women's house."

As she went out of the room to retrieve the file Heather smiled cheekily. "You never know what you may find in there!"

When she returned Rory was busy constructing a table with each of four names on it and spaces for information.

"What was it he asked of Lady Sara?"

Heather consulted the notes. "She was asked if she would tell Sir Thomas about her first marriage."

"And what was her reaction."

"She said it would probably kill him, she didn't think Charles knew what he was asking of her. Then she called him a bastard and stormed out of the house." Heather pouted her lips. "Not very ladylike of her was it?"

Rory looked up from his writing. "What do you think the reaction would be of Sir Thomas to Lady Sara's early indiscretions?"

Heather thought for a few moments. "Shock, disbelief, incredulity that she could be so stupid not to have realised the importance of the early marriage and the need to get it annulled. The position it puts him in. If there is any suggestion that the girls think Sara is only after their father's money, they could poison him against her. Sir Thomas is very frail at the moment; I would not like the responsibility of telling him his marriage is a sham."

"A women then with a lot to lose."

"She could be dangerous."

"I think then we should give her another 9."

"This isn't a competition you know."

Heather laughed. "I am glad you can joke about the possibility of both of us being murdered."

Rory looked up. "But the question is by whom?"

"I think the Colonel has the most to lose"

Rory moved papers around. "Right let's have a look at him."

"His whole status and life is tied up in being the Colonel."

"Could you imagine addressing him by his Christian name? What is it by the way?"

"Rodney I think." They both laughed.

Rory consulted his papers.

"He was asked to do something which would be incredibly difficult for him to do. To go and eat humble pie, to find the family of Pete Sanders, tell them the full story. How would they react? Would they just accept it and say no more? They could go to the Regiment and demand some sort of enquiry, even a court martial. The Colonel could be stripped not just of his medal but his whole status."

"I'm not sure he could live without being the Colonel you know."

"I think you're right. Is it a ten?"

"I think so Holmes. Next up is Peter."

Heather thought for a moment.

"His money is very precious to him."

"He doesn't look like a murderer to me."

"What Charles asked him to do would have been very hard for him to carry out and still remain in his position."

"He obviously likes the rich life."

"And so do his family. His wife was never short of expensive jewellery and even last winter at the carol service she out dressed Lady Sara, arriving in a long mink fur coat, the cost of which I dread to think of."

"All paid for from Miss Florence Merryweather's chest."

"Yes, I feel sorry for her. At least her name should be used as being a generous benefactor."

Heathers eyes narrowed. "It makes my blood boil to think of the times we have to bow and scrape to the Frobisher's as they gave their money to church projects."

"Not their money." interjected Rory.

"No. And I feel that Peter would not want to give it up without a fight".

"The love of money corrupts and Peter has shown just how much he loves it and by what means he has tried to preserve it"

"He must be 9."

"Now what about dear Hazel" said Rory. Charles wanted her to own up about who she really was and come clean."

Heather sighed. "That was asking a lot, she would be put in prison for deception and fraud."

She would also lose the farm to the American cousins and in her eyes tarnish the memory of her lover and companion Hazel."

"Wow, another ten for this one."

A look of exasperation came over Heathers features. "Is all this helping find the murderer Rory? We seem to be going round in circles. Each has their own strong motive and without something else we will never separate them."

Rory put his pen down. "Right let's talk about setting the trap."

"Progress at last. I will make a cup of tea."

When she returned Rory had a smile across his features. “I think I may have something we can start with.”

Heather smiled, “I knew I could always rely on my Dr. Watson.”

“Well.” said Rory. “Where do people get their biggest sources of gossip from in the village?”

“That’s obvious.” replied Heather. “Mrs Oaks in the village Post Office and PC. Plod in the Red Lion."

"Yes, just what I thought. Let’s use them to set the trap."

“Tomorrow morning go to the post office and enquire how you would send a confidential file to the Bishop’s Palace. What is the most secure way of sending it. Ask for a large envelope and what kind of secure proof of posting would be required. If there are other people in the post office, all the better. Ask about what time on Friday morning you have to deliver the package to the post office.”

Heather smiled. “That sounds like a good idea.” “I will also go into the Red Lion tonight and no doubt PC. Plod will be there. I will tell him in earshot of others, we have found a confidential file of Charles' in the study and we are sending it on Friday morning to the Bishop. You will be taking it to the Post Office for the 12 o’clock post.

He will pass on some comment but after I have left he will tell the others this titbit of gossip.”

Heather clapped her hands together. “That sounds a great plan, then what?”

“We wait and see what happens. I reckon each of the four will be closely monitoring what you are doing and any news they hear. Here comes the risky part. At 11 o'clock you set off for the post office. Walk along the road, it should take you about 15 minutes. There are houses around, it is in broad daylight, we will flush them out, and one of them will try to take the parcel. I could take the parcel if you wanted."

Heather looked at him. "No, Rory, I have to see this thing through. You forget that I took martial arts at the girl's college I went to, also I have done karate, quite useful for when boyfriends got out of hand. I think I can handle myself."

"Remember that the Colonel has a gun."

"I don't think he would try to use it in broad daylight in the village."

"There is also some more protection. I will go and fetch my motorbike in the morning from the flat. I can stay around 200 yards behind you and be with you quickly should something happen."

"That's a good idea; I will be safer knowing that you are so close."

The following morning, Heather walked to the Post Office. She didn't think she was observed or followed but you couldn't be sure.

There were a couple of people behind her in the queue when she got to counter.

"Oh! Mrs Oaks. How do I send a package, a file of papers to the Bishops palace? They are confidential and I want them to get there safely and quickly. What is the most secure way of sending them?"

Heather could see Mrs Oaks' nose twitch, a tasty bit of gossip this would be to be passed around the village. Sending confidential papers to the Bishop after the vicar has been found dead in the garden. A lot could be made of this.

Mrs Oaks leant forward in a confidential manner which Heather thought amusing. “I will sell you a large padded envelope today and you bring it back to me by 12 o’clock tomorrow and I will see that it goes special delivery in the lunchtime post and it will get to the Bishop the following morning.”

Heather bought the envelope and left the shop.

Rory went into the Red Lion in the evening and propping up the bar was in his usual place was PC.Burns surrounded by his usual cronies.

“How is the vicar’s wife?” He asked Rory.

“Oh she is bearing up very well in the circumstances I think. She has started sorting out the vicar’s study, she is sending some of the confidential papers she has found to the Bishop.”

“The vicar kept confidential papers then?” PC. Burns seemed impressed.

“Well you know, people tell him things, he keeps notes. It’s best that they are handled properly.”

PC.Burns. looked thoughtful. “Bit like my job really, you have to be able to keep confidences, the stories I could tell you. Did I ever tell you about the young curate we had here about twenty years ago who ran off with the butchers wife?” Rory felt it was his duty to listen to the story, one which he has heard many times before but one which seemed to get more embellishments the more it was told.

At last he felt he could leave, knowing that his story about the confidential papers would be all around the village by nightfall.

Both Rory and Heather were tense that evening? They couldn’t settle and any little noise or the phone ringing seemed to make them jump. They took extra precautions locking the house, windows locked and all doors double and triple locked. Heather went to bed early and Rory stayed up going over the plan and for tomorrow trying to work out every possibility, the last thing he wanted to do was put Heather in any form of danger.

Chapter Eleven

THE MORNING was bright and clear. After a quick breakfast Rory cycled back to his flat saying he would be back by 10am. He had been barely gone five minutes when the doorbell rang. Heather looked out from behind the curtains and saw Lady Sara's car in the drive. Her heart raced, was this it and so soon, without the protection of Rory, someone coming so early, they had not anticipated this. She put the door on the chain and opened it ajar.

Lady Sara looked imploringly at Heather.

"Can I come in; there is something I want to say."

Heather had a few seconds to make up her mind and opened the door.

Lady Sara came in and they went into the kitchen.

Heather noticed that Lady Sara was not her usual self! No make- up, her clothes were just jogging pants and a T-shirt. Her hair was unkempt and there were dark rings under her eyes.

"Heather, can I come straight to the point. I have to speak to you woman to woman. "

Heather was wary, she was not going to be taken in.

"Yes that is who we are. But I am one recently widowed. My husband's death is still unexplained and I need some answers."

"You have to believe me; I have had nothing to do with Charles' death. Yes, I confessed something to him which he only knew. It was something which if it became public knowledge would break my marriage apart and could take me to prison."

"I know." said Heather.

Lady Sara looked shocked. "The confidential papers, then it is true, Charles did make some notes and you have found them."

"Yes, and I've also read them."

There was an awkward silence.

"Then you will know that in my early life I did something which I thought at the time had no meaning."

"Let's not beat about the bush here Lady Sara, you were married in Barbados, and that marriage is still legal."

"Yes it is, and that's what I confessed to Charles."

"What do you want me do? Not send the papers to the Bishop? By the way how did you know I was going to do this?"

"The Post Office, Mrs Oaks told a member of my staff what your intentions were but she didn't realise I was involved."

Heather smiled to herself, then the plan was working, the village gossips were busy at work doing their business.

Sara looked imploringly at Heather. "Don't send the papers to the Bishop."

"Why shouldn't I?"

"Because..." Lady Sara took a deep breath, "I have thought about what Charles asked me do and I am going to do it tonight. I am going to come clean with Sir Thomas about my early marriage and tell him the truth."

Heather lent back in the chair considering what she had just heard.

"How can I believe what you are telling me is the truth?"

"You can speak to Sir Thomas tomorrow, I will tell him that you know and also how you know about me."

"And what of Charles' death or as I suspect murder?"

Lady Sara reached out and held Heathers hand! "You have to believe me I have taken no part in that. I was initially mad with Charles for what he asked me to do but as I thought about it I realised it was the only option. I love Thomas and I know he loves me. We are about to prove that love today when I tell him about my marriage in Barbados."

Heather looked into Lady Sara's eyes. "I do believe you Sara, you didn't murder Charles and don't worry what I have in this envelope." She patted the package on the table. "It is a lot of worthless parish correspondence; your secret will be safe with me."

Lady Sara broke down in tears. "Thank you Heather, I am not sure how I can repay you?"

"You can repay me by being honest with Sir Thomas! Have the courage to tell him everything. If your love is sound it will come through. It will be strong enough. God bless you."

With that they both hugged each other and Lady Sara left.

Half an hour later Rory returned. Initially he was perturbed that Lady Sara had visited without him being there to protect Heather.

"I shouldn't have left you alone. I blame myself. If anything had happened?"

Heather smiled at him. "Look Rory, nothing happened, in fact we have made progress, we have eliminated one of the suspects."

"How can you be sure?"

“Call it women’s intuition, but Lady Sara is no murderer. Foolish maybe, but she came to tell me she was going to do what Charles asked her to do. Does that sound like someone bent on murder at all costs and covering up her tracks? She is going to tell everything to Sir Thomas today and then she has said I can speak to him. She was only concerned if the Bishop had the papers it was another complication.”

Rory shrugged his shoulders. “I believe you, but you must understand we are playing a very dangerous game here, if you are right there is still one person who is prepared to kill to protect themselves.”

“I know.” said Heather “But what alternative do we have, call in the local police?”

They both laughed and Heather made them both a strong cup of coffee, she thought they may need it.

Chapter Twelve

AT ELEVEN o'clock prompt Heather set out from the vicarage to walk to the Post Office. A distance of about three-quarters of a mile she had done it so often but this was the first time she walked with such apprehension. She was carrying a large white Jiffy bag, taped up and with the Bishops name and address in large letters on the front. What the Bishop would make of it if he ever received it was anyone's guess as it just contained a bundle of various parish papers and correspondence of no great importance.

Heather started walking down the hill towards the church. There was no-one on the road and after she had gone twenty yards she heard the reassuring roar of Rory's motorbike from the rear.

A lorry came up the hill towards her and she had to step off the road into the verge. She walked on, alert to anyone who was around. Then, from round a bend a large tractor came round the bend towards her, as it came closer she realised the driver was Hazel Forrest. She had a strange look on her face. Heather felt herself tensing up and a shiver running down her spine. He mind raced, something they had not thought of, a vehicle hitting her and then when she was on the ground someone snatching the parcel.

The tractor came on, moving slowly, the huge front wheels could easily kill her thought Heather, then just when she thought she should jump into the hedge the tractor was past her and she saw Hazel, tears streaming down her cheeks holding fast to the wheel as it carried on past her.

After it passed, she was trembling and wondering how wise it was for her to do this, but now it was too late, she walked on towards the church and noticed a figure standing underneath the wooden front lintel gate. It was a man and he was looking out on to the road, as she got closer she realised it was the Colonel. She almost froze and wasn't sure how she managed to continue walking.

The church was on the opposite side of the road and slowly the realisation occurred that Rory would not see the Colonel, he was hidden by the gate, he would not realise she was in danger. What should she do, cry out? Run for all she was worth? She didn't know how she did it but she very calmly carried on walking and when she drew level noticed there was something strange about the Colonel. He was dressed in his dark blue blazer, but he had his regimental cap on and what's more, a row of medals on his lapel. His hand moved to his side pocket and Heather went cold, where was Rory she thought? Why hadn't he come like they had arranged. Her mouth went dry.

She tried to continue walking and then a curious thing happened. The Colonel clicked his heels together, gave a salute to Heather, turned quickly and marched down the path into church? Heather could only stop and watch open mouthed at this unusual display. It was probably this that distracted her and she didn't see the red jaguar come round the bend and head straight towards her. At the last moment she saw it as it was almost upon her, the only thing she saw in a blur was the murderous figure of Peter Frobisher hunched up over the wheel as he bore down upon her. She moved quickly and jumped into the ditch at the side of the road, landing on her side. The car screeched to a halt and Peter Frobisher jumped out and ran towards Heather. He pulled her upright and she realised he was brandishing a knife. He demanded that she handed over the package which now lay in the ditch. He was red faced and obviously had been drinking.

"The package, you stupid bitch, let me have the package."

Heather looked at him, anger welling up inside her as she realised she was confronting her husband's murderer. Then a number of things all happened at once.

There was a gunshot from the church tower which momentarily meant that Peter Frobisher looked towards the church. Heather seized her chance and with one kick lashed out and hit his wrist, he dropped the knife, cursing as he did so, clutching his injured hand. He didn't see or hear the Motorbike bearing down on him or see the baseball bat wielded by Rory who struck Peter Frobisher full in the ribs, probably breaking three or four of them. He crumpled to the ground clutching his side and moaning loudly. By then the Ladies Flower Arranging Group were running out of church screaming and people were streaming out of the Red Lion, PC. Burns was trying to button up his tunic as he ran towards the commotion.

For a few minutes bedlam seemed to reign before the sirens of police cars converged on the scene from all directions and two ambulances arrived. Heather was by now sitting on the grass verge being comforted by Rory and others from the village.

Peter Frobisher was lying in a crumpled heap in the ditch moaning and clutching his sides, his face contorted with rage and pain and looking over at Heather.

The police cars and Ambulances roared to a halt and some order was quickly established. Peter Frobisher was taken away in an Ambulance still muttering and complaining he was the innocent party. The Ambulance was given a Police Escort.

Two other Ambulance men were carrying a stretcher out of the church with the body of the Colonel lying upon it covered by a red blanket. They stopped just before Heather. One of the Ambulance men spoke to PC.Burns. "There was a note left by the side of the body to a Heather Jowett."

PC.Burns said in a voice trying to take command of a situation which was well beyond him said, "I'll take care of that, it will be valuable evidence."

Heather snatched it from his grasp. "Not before I've read it, as it is addressed to me."

She tore open the envelope.

It was written in long-hand in black ink. In big capital letters and with today's date on it were written.

PLEASE REGARD THIS AS MY LAST WILL AND TESTAMENT.

Dear Heather,

I wanted to write to you and explain a few things and hopefully put something right in my life which I should have done a long time ago.

Your husband Charles was a good man and didn't deserve what happened to him.

You have to understand, I did not kill him, it wasn't me, you have to believe me.

He was right in what he asked me to do. The only thing is my pride stopped me from doing it. By the time you read this you will know I have taken the coward's way out and shot myself.

I couldn't face the shame and the humiliation of people knowing that I am not the person I have tried to be. I don't deserve their respect but I know I couldn't face their questions and accusations.

I allowed a great injustice to take place and for that I know my name will be stripped of its association with valour and courage and forever be linked to deceit and cowardice. I know I deserve that.

Please can you do something for me? I would like you to go and find the family of Lieutenant Pete Sanders, I think he came from the North-East - the regiment will have his details. Take my medals and all the money I have, I leave to his family. Give it to them. Let them take a trip to France to see their son's grave and let it be marked a hero's grave. Tell them the story of their son's great heroism. Tell them it was stolen from him and the person who did it bitterly regrets his actions.

I have tried to serve my fellows, the church and the people of this village to the best of my ability. I am sorry for the shame I have brought upon it...

The Colonel [who was)

Heather folded up the letter and handed it back to PC.Burns. She turned to Rory! Can we go back to the vicarage it's been quite a day, I feel really tired.

All through the afternoon, people called and more police arrived to take statements, this time Heather and Rory were believed. It was a tiring day for both of them but there was a sense of justice being done and been seen to be done.

PC.Burns held forth as usual that night in the Red Lion. But somehow his boasts and knowledge of all the facts and suspicions didn't ring true. Certainly his superiors would have some questions to ask him about his earlier investigations and the wrong conclusions he came to.

Heather's sister Joyce arrived fussing around as usual and made Rory and Heather some supper before Rory left on his motorcycle. Heather thanked Rory for all his help and reflected "It had been quite a day for Sherlock Holmes and Dr Watson." Joyce wondered what on earth her sister was talking about.

Postscript

A FEW WEEKS later Rory and Heather took the train to Gateshead and found Pete Sanders family. An old couple in their eighties, they didn't know how to receive the news of their sons heroism. His mother said. "I knew he was a hero, he was always a hero in my heart and now you have just confirmed it." The War Office replaced the medals with ones specially stuck for him and the Colonel's money paid for them to go to France first-class to see their son's grave.

A few weeks after the incident. A small wedding ceremony took place in the church at dawn attended by Sir Thomas and Lady Hethrington. The only witnesses were Heather and a close friend of Sara's, Rory took the service. This was of course after Sara had managed to get the first marriage in Barbados annulled. The Registry office and Police had been very understanding and were not going to press charges. Sir Thomas lived for another year and he and Lady Sara were very happy together.

What of Peter Frobisher? The Law Society did a thorough investigation, and he was struck off. The court found him guilty of the murder of Charles Jowett and attempted murder of Heather Jowett, also theft, fraud and deception. He is serving a full life sentence in Durham jail. His assets were confiscated and he didn't put anything in his wife's name so she had to forfeit her jewellery and the fur coats not to mention the car and the two houses.

Shortly afterwards she left the Village. A very wise judge ordered that Peter Frobisher's assets of over two million pounds which were traced should go into a special trust fund to be called the Merryweather-Jowett memorial fund and to be used for charitable purposes. The trustees were to be Heather, Rory and Sir Thomas and Lady Hethrington.

What of Hazel Forrest? Heather and Rory met her and they agreed on a plan of action, as they were the only people who knew the real truth.

Rory and Heather asked Hazel to set up the Farm as a Charitable Trust which would benefit the village and the workers at the Farm. Hazel could live in the Farmhouse as long as she lived and then it would be handed over to the Trust. Hazel was overjoyed and thanked them both. Before she left, Heather had a question for her.

"Did you set out on that Friday morning to kill me with the Tractor?"

Hazel hesitated before answering. "I'm not sure what I was thinking, I set out with that intention, yes, I couldn't lose the farm to those money-grabbing cousins, it seemed so wrong. But when I saw you I realised it was also wrong to harm you. I couldn't do it, I just carried on down the road crying like a child."

They all hugged each other and Heather and Rory promised to keep Hazel's secret safe.

What became of Heather and Rory? Then read on.

THE SECOND EPISTLE

Chapter Thirteen

THE BISHOP'S waiting room was a very uncomfortable place. Maybe deliberately so, thought Rev Rory Coverdale as he perched on the long pew that took up one side of the wall. Opposite him, as if looking down on in judgement were paintings of previous Bishops each looking more formidable and sterner than the previous one, thought Rory.

The door opened at the far end of the room and the Bishop's secretary came in, a small middle-aged women with her hair held up in a bun, she looked as formidable as some of the Bishops on the wall. "The Bishop will see you now." Her tone relayed the message that he shouldn't be too long and it was a great privilege he was being called to see his Lordship. He was ushered into a small corridor with more pictures of long-dead clergy, the door at the end was open and it was large palatial room containing large oak bookcases and a very large desk behind which the Bishop stood with his back to the door looking out of the window towards the garden.

He motioned for Rory to take a seat and the Secretary quietly left the room. He turned to face Rory, and he realised the Bishop looked none too pleased.

"I am quite lost for words Coverdale. I don't know what to say. In all my years as a Bishop I have never come across anything like this. Can you please explain your behaviour?"

Rory looked quizzically at the Bishop. "My behaviour, my Lord?"

The Bishop turned around him and faced him, his face red with anger, the veins on his neck purple and standing out. "Yes, your behaviour Coverdale. A good vicar dies in the parish and he's hardly been dead five minutes, not even buried and I am hearing stories about how you are comforting the widow and living in the vicarage. The whole village is scandalised. If the parish hasn't had enough to go through, with the suicide of the church warden, then the murder of the vicar, not to mention the attempted murder of the vicar's wife. And then you taking advantage of the situation to seduce his wife. I believe I am due an explanation!"

Rory was amazed at the outburst and spoke up. " I have not seduced Heather. I was only doing what I thought was right. Heather needed and asked for my help; it was both of us you may remember that helped catch the murderer."

The Bishop was not used to being answered back, at least not by curates. "That may be so but it does not give you the excuse to take advantage of the situation with a grieving widow who is looking for support."

"Have you spoken to Heather?"

"No, I don't think it is necessary and I don't need you telling me how to conduct my investigations young man. It is quite clear to me you have become too close and this matter must be addressed to prevent any scandal."

Rory's jaw dropped open; he could only stare at the Bishop open-mouthed. The Bishop continued.

"I have decided to suspend you forthwith from Parish duties and however laudable you think your actions have been I cannot have scandal in the parish. I am sending you away, as far away as I can; there is a parish in Cornwall which is looking for a curate. You will take up your duties there at the earliest opportunity. My secretary Mrs. Jones will give you the details and who to contact on your way out." The Bishop resumed his previous posture of standing looking out into the garden.

Rory was still shocked and couldn't believe what he was hearing. Since the night of the robbery Rory had not stayed at the vicarage. He had been very careful not to get too close to Heather and was dismayed at what he'd heard, village tittle tattle and it seemed the Bishop was not interested in hearing his side of the story. Would he have been believed anyway? If he had told the Bishop the truth would he have accepted it? It seemed so fantastic.

Rory stood up and faced the back of the Bishop.

"No Bishop, I'm not going to Cornwall or anywhere else you may want to send me. I have done nothing wrong. You haven't even bothered to establish the facts."

The Bishop turned to face Rory his features growing redder by the second.

"Such impertinence, I will not have it, and from a curate! You will go and are fortunate I am giving you a new position. You could be put under discipline and even de-frocked because of your behaviour. Those are my orders young man and you would do well to heed them and be grateful."

Rory was standing next to the Bishop.

"You can keep your position Bishop, I am not

going to Cornwall, I am resigning as a priest from the Church of England."

With that Rory turned and went out of the room slamming the door as he went which drew a shocked look from the Bishop's Secretary.

He returned to his flat in Little Stanbury and began to pack, he was unsure where he would go, perhaps his sister would put him up for a few weeks, she lived about sixty miles away. He kicked his motorbike into life and for the last time roared down the lane to the vicarage.

Heather was there by herself. Rory went in and immediately Heather sensed something was wrong. "What's happened Rory?"

"I have resigned as a priest."

She gave him a hug as tears fell from his eyes.

He told her the full story of the meeting with the Bishop over a cup of coffee and Heather could only blame herself.

Heather was distraught. "It's my fault all this, it was me who wanted you to stay. I will go and see the Bishop and tell him the truth. It's my entire fault, what a mess I have caused. But you mustn't resign, Rory you are a good priest, you have done nothing wrong."

Rory looked at her, his voice quiet but with a firm determination.

"You know when I was speaking with the Bishop I realised something which was very important to me. As important to my calling to the church, Heather, I love you."

Heather at first looked shocked then a smile came across her face.

"Rory, I know it is too soon but I think I love

you as well. My feelings for you are very special but what are we going to do? It's too soon, my emotions are all over the place, it wouldn't be fair to make long term plans and commitments."

They embraced together and kissed.

Rory did go and stay with his sister Florence who was very supportive. He got a job as a supply teacher in a local school. He never lost his sense of vocation and joined the local Methodist Church, helping out at their services and enjoying a more relaxed sense of churchmanship. He stayed in contact with Heather and wrote every week, his letters were chatty and fun always something new at school to tell her or what was happening at the church.

As the weeks went by she began to rebuilt her life, she realised that she would have to leave the vicarage soon, they were already looking for another vicar and kind as people were she could only stand so much of being looked upon as the grieving widow. She would have liked to know who had gone to the Bishop, she never did find out but she wondered if the village shop and Mrs Oaks had been the culprit. Not only providing a useful means of telling the four suspects and setting the trap, but also providing suspicions about Rory and Heather's relationship. Had Heather betrayed Charles? She agonised long and hard over that difficult question over the next few weeks, with many sleepless nights.

Then one morning she woke up and felt different. She went around the vicarage packing things up, sending things to the charity shop, throwing other things away and putting all she was going to keep together. She realised that she was ready to move on, but where and what would she do?

Heather stayed at the vicarage another three months until the new vicar was appointed. She then left Little Stanbury and went to stay in London with her sister to find time to look at what the future would hold and what she would do.

Rory and Heather met in London one weekend. It was the first time they had met since Rory had left the church. Now was the time when both of them felt free to be themselves and they found each other's company stimulating and both wanted more. They went to the theatre, shared meals and went for long walks in the parks. They continued to meet over the next few months and gradually their feelings for each other became more evident and Rory proposed. Heather hesitated, she was unsure about the age difference, some 10 years! Would he still love her when she was old? She was past child-bearing age; Rory would be giving up too much. No, he was sure and he had another surprise for her, he wanted to re-enter the church, not as an Anglican priest but as a Methodist Minister. He had been having conversations and it would be relatively easy to transfer and apply for the Methodist ministry, he could even do his training part-time fitting in with his school teaching duties.

Fourteen months after the death of Charles Jowett, Heather and Rory were married in the small Methodist church in Duxford. There were a few raised eyebrows in Little Stanbury and it was the cause celebre in the Post Office and the Red Lion for a few days but life moves on. Most people wished the couple well. There were letters and presents from both Lady Sara and Hazel Forrest. There was a grunt from the Bishop when he heard the news.

After a number of interviews with the Methodist Church including one with both of them, Rory was accepted and after six months part time training they were ready to go out into circuit as a married couple. The Methodist Church stationed their ministers so it would be an appointment chosen by the church. When they heard the suggestion, they were both pleased, a market town in rural Yorkshire, what could be better?

First though, was the honeymoon. They thought about a holiday with sun and relaxing by a pool, but realised that it didn't really suit them, they would like something a bit more like an adventure. Heather came up with the suggestion after watching a programme on television. Why not Norway? A trip on a cruise ship, the postal express up the Norwegian Coast to the Arctic Circle. As soon as Heather suggested it to Rory, he was smitten. He had always wanted to experience the Arctic Circle and this would be a special holiday. They started planning and looking forward to what would be a very unexpected and exciting honeymoon that neither of them could have dreamt of.

The trip to Bergen was special, a night at sea when they could at last share their dreams and hopes together. The cruise would be on a working boat dropping into the small ports and harbours up the coast and the boat was small enough and intimate, not like the huge liners sailing around the Mediterranean. They both knew they had good sea legs and even a storm at sea didn't spoil their enjoyment.

They were both up early and out on deck as

their ship entered the harbour at Bergen. Although a city it had all the charm and atmosphere of a small town which they were keen to explore. The harbour was busy with ships of various sizes loading and unloading their cargoes. They booked into their hotel near the harbour and went exploring to see the delights of Bergen.

They came across the peaceful haven of Lill Lungegardsvann, a beautiful lake surrounded by parkland and trees. The rhododendrons were out in all their splendour and as they walked hand in hand through the parkland they both felt at peace with each other and the world unaware of the storm clouds gathering in the north.

The Lake opened onto the Festplassen, the city's festival square where a small orchestra was playing excerpts from Norway's most foremost composer Edvard Greig.

That night they enjoyed a trip on the funicular railway to the top of Mt. Floyen named after the weather–vane at it's summit. They went up at sunset and stayed until it was dark marvelling at the views of Bergen, the sun sinking over the sea as the city lights were turned on.

They stood together and embraced in front of the weather-vane which had stood there for centuries, showing wind strength and direction for the benefit of sailors entering and leaving the harbour below. It has been blown down, burnt down even torn down, but each time it has been rebuilt.

"A bit like what we've just committed to" said Rory, "Nothing can separate us...for better and for worse..." Heather smiled and gave his hand a big squeeze. There love would be tested on their honeymoon voyage in a way they could not have guessed.

DAY ONE...The voyage begins from Bergen

The following morning they took a brief taxi ride from their hotel to the harbour to find their ship, The SS Lofoten to begin their adventure on the coastal express boat.

The coastal express boat is a unique experience of cruising. The Hurtigruten vessels have been calling at the 34 ports on the coast since 1893. Many of the ports of call along the way are little more than tranquil hamlets on tiny islands. The inhabitants rely on the ships to bring essential groceries and supplies or take passengers to the larger towns. Other ports of call are long-established, bustling towns, where the boat stays longer enabling passengers to take excursions.

The ship was all it should be, not too big but a size which was intimate enough to get to know yet big enough to lose yourself without tripping over the same people all the time. They had an outside cabin with a small pothole which looked out to sea. They were also treating themselves to first-class accommodation.

The food was delicious, breakfast and lunch were buffet style and what a selection. The table simply groaned with selections of fresh fish, cooked meats, different breads, pastries and other delightful Norwegian fare.

Dinners were more formal, the seating was allocated and Heather and Rory were given a table of four with them lves, an American lady,

Cara who had travelled the world and liked to let everyone know where she had been. Her husband had died a few years before and obviously left her a huge fortune which she used to see new places, this was the latest leg of her trip. Then there was a small wiry man, Peter who was an antiquarian book dealer, he was very quiet and Rory thought he would have an interesting story. If only he would be confident to tell it.

The first night they all shared a couple of bottles of wine and talked about their hopes for the voyage. For Rory and Heather it was to see the sights and scenes of the Arctic, to enjoy their honeymoon together and see it as a great adventure. For Cara it was another cruise, she was there to see what delights Norway had in store for her, to meet new friends and see a penguin. Peter had to tell her that penguins are only found at the South Pole and there are none at the North Pole. They all laughed as Cara said “Well, I will have to go south after this cruise.” As for Peter, he was a little reticent to share his hopes, he talked generally about looking forward to taking the ‘coastal express’ and seeing new places. Then he said something which made everyone at the table sit up and listen more intently. He was also there to remember friends who had died. He was there to go back to a place he had been in the Second World War. It would be twenty five years ago when the other men in his platoon had been executed by the German Gestapo. He was going back to pay his respects. After he had told his story there was a silence, thankfully broken by the Norwegian steward coming to serve coffee. The talk was then about the ship and the table quickly broke up and everyone went their separate ways.

Rory and Heather went up on deck, the light was almost fading, the boat ploughing a gentle furrow through the waters, the shoreline with the hills shrouded in low cloud and some with snow lining the crevasses.

Rory turned to Heather quizzically. “What do you make of our table companions?”

Heather rested her arms on the rails and gazed out to sea. “I like them, Cara is just what an American should be. I don’t know why they want to go and see the world. I always think you can divide Americans into two groups, the ones who never leave the shores of the U.S.A, don’t have a passport and see no need for one. Then there are others who feel the world needs to know about America and want to go and tell the world.”

“What about Peter?”

“I don’t know, he looked frightened when he told us that story. Why is he going there now? Surely there can be nothing to frighten him now? I also think that he wasn’t telling us the full story.”

“Neither did we! We didn’t tell them about Charles’ murder, or of how we met and how we solved his murder!”

“That’s for another day. There is nothing wrong with being economical with the truth.” Heather gave Rory a playful nudge in the ribs.

At that moment the ships hooter sounded. A large deep bass sound and they both laughed and hugged each other.

Walking back they noticed the hot tub on the deck.

“I must have a go in that.” Heather said going

across and feeling the temperature of the water. Rory shivered. "But what about when you get out, won't it be freezing cold?"

Heather laughed. "You just have to run fast that's all."

With that Heather raced off around the deck leaving Rory smiling as he watched her as she disappeared around the stern and onto the rear deck. He resumed his position of leaning across the rail and looking at the scene. They were slowly approaching a small quay and he could see tiny figures on the shore and a few motor vehicles. He watched as the ship manoeuvred around and slipped effortlessly into the mooring, something which the Captain must have done many times before.

A rope was thrown from the stern and then hauled around the capstan, a similar process was being done at the prow. As the engines died Heather returned breathless, her hair a tangle, face flushed and looking wonderful. Rory held her tight and kissed her. "I needed that" said Heather. They both laughed and held each other close.

They watched over the rail as 50 feet below them the passenger ramp was pushed forward out of the boat and the same was done with a small cargo ramp. A few passengers disembarked and others boarded the boat. A small fork-lift truck set to work, first taking pallets of cargo off the boat and then loading up half a dozen pallets which were on the quayside. All was done efficiently and in a few minutes the loud siren again sounded and the ropes were cast adrift as the boat slowly edged it's way out of the quay. This was a process which would be repeated over 40 times in the next ten days as the SS Lofoten went into various ports, sometimes staying for a few minutes, other times a few hours, leaving time for sight-seeing and visits on the shore.

Heather and Rory went inside hand in hand, as they passed the bar they heard music. "Shall we go in for a few minutes?" asked Rory.

I look a real mess let me go and have a shower first said Heather. "I will join you as soon as I can."

Rory went into the bar and ordered a beer, there was a pianist playing and singing popular songs. There were a few people scattered around the room and Rory sat at an empty table. The musician was good, obviously English and his repartee was extensive from the fifties classics to the modern groups. Rory found himself tapping his foot to the tunes and relaxing thinking how much he was enjoying life and how good it was.

The only blemish was a small group of German men who seemed to be drinking huge quantities of lager and were very loud, ignoring the music and laughing and talking amongst themselves.

After about twenty minutes Heather slipped into the seat next to Rory. She looked stunning, she was wearing a black dress which complemented her figure and she had done her hair in the way which Rory had never noticed before. She had put on some jewellery and her perfume smelled exquisite. Rory leant close and whispered in her ear.

"I still prefer you hot and sweaty"

Heather smiled and suddenly Rory felt his leg being nipped which meant he let out a loud yelp which drew stares from the rest of the audience.

"That'll teach you not to give a lady proper compliments."

They both laughed.

They stayed there for quite a time, getting up to dance and really enjoying themselves. The musician readily played their suggestions and they had a very good night.

As they returned to their room hand in hand, Rory looked at Heather.

"I really did enjoy that, I hope the rest of the voyage is as good."

"Yes" said Heather, "I enjoyed it too except the comments from those Germans."

Rory looked puzzled. "I never heard them say anything?"

"You didn't teach German, I understood every comment they made. I didn't realise my bottom made such a good impression."

Rory looked aghast. "If you had told me I would have said something to them."

Heather smiled. "Don't worry, I can cope with men's comments, they were just so crude and they obviously thought I couldn't understand."

Rory slapped Heathers bottom lightly. "It is one of your best assets you know"

Heather smiled. "And what are your best assets Rev. Coverdale?"

They had now reached their room.

"I think you will have to find out."

"I wonder how I will do that Rev Coverdale?"

DAY TWO...Maloy to Kristiansund

It was a late breakfast that Heather and Rory enjoyed. The array of food was extremely appetising and they were soon tucking in with great abandon. Cold meats, fish, cheeses, all kinds of fruit, as well as a cooked breakfast, cereals and an array of fresh bread.

They sat at a window table looking out at the ever changing scenery as the boat manoeuvred between the narrow fjords and were pleased that they had chosen the perfect honeymoon, but had they?

They were joined at the table by Peter who only had a large mug of black coffee. They couldn't persuade him to have anything else and he looked very troubled.

"I shouldn't have come on this voyage it has been a huge mistake."

They both looked puzzled. "But why?" asked Rory. "Surely you can relax a bit and enjoy the scenery and the ship, I know the purpose of your trip is very sad, but you are doing it for your friends, who if they knew would be so pleased."

Peter lent closer to them at the table so that they could not be overheard.

"I think I have been recognised."

Heather and Rory looked puzzled.

"What do you mean?" asked Heather, "Who has recognised you?"

"I can't talk here but I need to trust someone else on this ship, can you come to my cabin in half an hour, make sure no-one sees you and I mean no-one, not even the cleaning staff or any members of the crew."

Rory said. "Yes, we will help if we can but..."

Before he could ask his question, Peter was off, walking out of the dining room nervously looking around him.

Rory turned to Heather. "What do you make of that Sherlock?"

Heather looked quizzically at Rory. "I thought we were on honeymoon Watson."

"We are, but we can't refuse a plea for help can we?"

They both smiled, but it was a nervous smile as both of them were not sure what they were getting themselves into.

Half an hour later Rory and Heather went to Peter's cabin. He had helpfully written the number on the menu at the table. They had to abort their visit twice because of another passenger in the corridor outside the cabin and then a cleaning girl in the corridor. As she went into one of the cabins Rory and Heather quickly went up to Peter's cabin and knocked.

There was a nervous voice inside. "Who is it?"

"It's us, Rory and Heather."

Peter quickly opened the door and they slipped in. He looked out into the corridor to make sure they were not observed.

Peter motioned them to sit on the spare bunk. Peter sat down and brought a large handkerchief out of his pocket, he mopped his brow as he was sweating.

They faced each other across the small cabin and Heather looked intently at Peter studying his features trying to work out what had disturbed him so much. He was a small wiry man, obviously strong with good shoulders and muscles on his arms, he had been used to doing manual work. He had a small face which reminded Heather of a small animal, one which at the moment looked very frightened and hunted.

Rory broke the silence.

"I don't understand what is happening Peter, how can we help you, are you in some sort of danger? We could always go to the Captain."

Peter looked distraught. "No, no you can't do that, just listen to my story and see if you believe me and once you have heard it, you have to promise me that if you decide not to help me you will forgot everything I have told you and not tell anyone."

Rory looked puzzled. "Why did you choose us?"

Peter smiled for the first time that morning. "You are a clergyman. You understand other people's confidences; also from our first meeting I liked both of you. You both seem strong characters."

"Thank you." said Rory "You can trust us and we have some experience of dealing with difficult situations and getting through them" he cast a glance to Heather who raised an eyebrow.

Peter got up and went to the dressing table. "Would you like a drink? I will need one to tell my story." He picked up a bottle of whiskey.

"It's very early in the morning." said Rory.

"Yes two small ones with a little water." said Heather as she took charge.

Peter poured the drinks, handed them round and then sat down. He took a large gulp of whiskey and began to speak.

"Have you ever heard of the Shetland Bus?"

Rory looked puzzled. Heather spoke up. “Yes, it happened during the war when Norway was occupied by Germany. It was a means of taking people and cargo to Norway using their fishing boats. They went from Shetland I believe; it was a very successful operation.”

Rory looked admiringly at Heather.

“Yes” said Peter. “You are correct. It was run for many years and the Germans became desperate to stop it but it proved a vital supply link to the Norwegian resistance and also a way of getting agents into Norway and finding out what the Germans were doing.

It had been running a couple of years when I became involved. You see, during the war I was an explosive expert. Blowing things up was my speciality. It’s harder than you think. Some people think you just have to plant an explosive and bang, it blows up and you get away. There is a lot more to it than that. You have to calculate the amount of explosives you need and more importantly where to place them. You also need timers to be able to get away and need to deploy them so that they will not be found before the explosion. There is a lot of expertise in blowing things up and if you get it wrong you pay the price with your life.”

Heather took a gulp of the warm amber whiskey.

“The Shetland Bus operated from Lunna in the Shetland Isles. I was sent there to help with the explosives and train the men who would go to the mainland, usually Norwegians to blow up the installations the Germans were building. Also, hampering them and tying down troops in Norway. I was there for three years and all went well, it hindered the Germans no end. There was always something they had to look out for, repair or build again. But the Norwegians paid a heavy price. There were collaborators who informed on the saboteurs, many were captured and killed. The Gestapo began to get very angry, threatening the civilian population about giving up the Norwegians who were helping the British. It all started to get very nasty."

He looked away out of the porthole to the hills and small settlements clinging to the sides of the mountains.

"We started losing more men and also the civilians were paying a heavy price. The Germans were getting stronger and as you can see the Norwegian Coast is ideal for U.boats and the German fleet. They could come out of the fjords and hunt down Allied ships seemingly with impunity. When Russia entered the war we had to send convoys around the Norwegian Coast to help supply the Russians in their fight against Germany. The battleship Tirpitz was stationed in Norway and the U-Boats continued to do so much damage.

It was then I was asked to go to London. I wondered what it was all about. I had to go to a series of meetings at the War Office, they wanted to hit the German U-Boats hard in Norway, and they couldn't do it from the air as the installations were too well defended. Overland attacks and parachuting troops in was out of the question because of the mountainous terrain. It had to be by sea and the way chosen was by the Shetland Bus.

They then showed me the maps and photographs of the new U-boat base at Altafjorden asking if it could be breached, how much explosive would be required and how such an operation could take place.

We discussed it for three days with all the experts at the War Office. Eventually we came up with a plan. Only a very few people would know what the operation was. It would be disguised right up to the last minute so as to minimise the chance of betrayal.

We worked out that we would have to send four boats packed with explosives and the resistance fighters would store it on the mainland at four different points. Each of the boats would be unaware of the other boats. We could trust the Norwegian sailors but their families and friends we were not so sure of.

I was to hand-pick a group of five other explosive experts who I would train in Lunna before going on the Shetland Bus and meeting up with the most senior of the Norwegian resistance.

We would make our way to Altafjorden and plant our explosives. We would have six hours to escape, a boat would be waiting for us and it would take us two hours overland from the submarine base to the boat. If all went well we would be on open sea before the explosion. If it didn't, well you can guess what the result would have been."

Heather took another gulp which drained her glass, Peter very helpfully filled the glasses again.

Peter gave a long sigh. "The rest of the story is not that easy to tell.

We trained together the six of us, north of Lunna on the small island of Unst. We practised climbing the local cliffs with ropes, improving our small boat skills and with the help of the local RAF base practised laying the explosives.

When the boats with the explosives had departed

for Norway we went to Lunna to wait their return. After five days they all returned safely, each bringing good news and also people who needed to get to England. There were Secret Agents whose cover had been blown, recruits for the Norwegian air-force as well as some women and children."

Peter looked reflective. "War is a strange time. No-one at Lunna asked why six Englishman were there, no-one asked what the operation was for, only the Commander knew. Knowledge can be dangerous, in wartime, the less you know the better. At last, we were ready to go. The Norwegian captain and his three man crew were handpicked and the best. We set off early one evening under the cover of darkness. The North Sea was quite rough and a few of the men had difficulty coping with the rolling of the small boat and were quite seasick, something which amused the Norwegian crew.

We arrived off the Norwegian Coast and acted like any of the many hundreds of Norwegian fishing vessels, we kept below deck as there were planes overhead checking for any unusual activity on the fishing boats. All day we bobbed around off the coast, we could see from the small porthole the occasional U boat, on it's way out to sea or returning to it's pen. There were also German destroyers and frigates. Every time one came close we lay still thinking that if they asked to board us and search the ship we were finished. We were with a whole group of other fishing vessels and apart from having to get out of the way of the German ships the day passed without incident.

As darkness fell we headed away from the other

vessels and towards the shore. The skipper picked a small inlet, which was just wide enough for a fishing boat, anything bigger would struggle to navigate the narrow channel. We landed on a deserted shore with only a few buildings on the shoreline which looked like fishing sheds. There were a few men waiting for us; The Norwegian Resistance. Their English was very good and they told us they had all the explosives together now, all in one building, they pointed to the far shed. I looked at Andy one of the other explosive experts and we smiled. There was enough TNT in that building to blow up the Houses of Parliament and half the buildings around it.

We went in to examine it, it was fine, nice and dry and besides we had brought the detonators and timers, so it was quite safe!

We quickly dispersed the explosives amongst the Norwegians and ourselves, each of us taking a heavy load on our back as well as a bag to carry. Altogether there would 12 of us. The six Norwegians would help carry the explosives into the pen and then leave us to deploy them. After we had done our job we would leave to come back to our rendezvous point. There we would be picked up by the fishing boat.

We then set off, first by lorry and then when we got closer we disembarked and went on foot around the headland. Because of the rough terrain the U boat pen would not be defended strongly from the land side. If there was going to be an attack it would be from the air, it would be madness to come around the cliffs, the path was treacherous and only fit for sheep. The path had been checked a few days before by the Resistance and found to be navigable, if a little difficult.

The night had started clear but now there was rain which made the walking miserable and we all knew when it came to the cliffs they would be treacherous.

The rain came down in torrents to make the paths muddy and slippery, the only consolation was that it would be a keen guard indeed who would be out and about on such an evening. The path was difficult enough but along with the rucksack on the back of each man plus the bag they were carrying, it was slow and painful progress along the side of the cliff, the waters of the North Sea breaking below us. As we finally reached the headland and began to go inland the wind and rain were behind us but now we had a new danger, the lights of the U boat base ahead.

The U Boat base at Altafjorden had been recently constructed and was one of the biggest on the Norwegian coast. Because of it's location it was ideally situated to strike at the Russian convoys and the U-boats were having a devastating effect on them. Hundreds of thousands of tons of shipping and hundreds of men had already been lost and the Allies had seemingly no answer to what the Germans were throwing at them.

At last we made it to the base and surveyed the scene, there must have been thirty U-Boats in the pens, being the middle of the night the guards were sparse and probably sleeping. It was heavily guarded from the road but from the sea, hardly anything. We crept around the headland and made our way into the base from the sea. There were two guards which the Norwegians took care of, careful not to make a noise.

We reached the base and split up to attach the explosives, each man knew what he had to do and how he would do it, we had practised for weeks. The six Norwegians wished us well and left us, returning back up the cliff path.

Within an hour the job was done and after setting the timers we began to head back around the cliff, moving faster now with no heavy loads to weigh us down. The lorry was waiting for us and within an hour we had reached the beach and the rendezvous point. It was there when it began to go wrong. We saw the lights of a boat coming towards us and too late realised it wasn't a fishing boat but a German launch. We turned to flee up the single track road only to find three German jeeps and numerous motorbikes coming down the hill. We were surrounded, with few weapons we were outgunned, we were finished. We were captured and taken inside the large shed and tied up. It was then that the Gestapo arrived. There was a large, ugly looking man in the characteristically black uniform with two of his henchmen. They roughed us up then started asking the questions, what we doing there, had we planted explosives at the U-Boat base? What time were they due to go off? Of course we didn't say anything, other than our name, rank and number. This angered them and they got very nasty. There was a radio and one of them was in touch with the submarine base. It was obvious they couldn't find the explosives. We weren't surprised as they weren't where they would expect to find them. We hadn't placed them on the boats. In London we had looked at a geological survey of the cave where the boats were moored. It was a natural cave but the rocks around here are of a certain brittleness and a well-placed explosive would bring the whole roof down. They were well hidden in the roof.

As the minutes ticked by the Gestapo got more and more desperate, but we didn't give them anything, they were bastards. Sorry ma'am, as he looked towards Heather. I won't tell you what they did, but in some of my dreams or should I say nightmares I can still hear the screams."

Heather and Rory both took large sips of the whiskey.

"Eventually they were getting desperate, so they did their worst. They took one aside and said they would shoot him if we didn't tell them where the explosives were. They shot him. They repeated this five times until I was the only one left. Then it happened. A huge roar and the sky lit up, I knew we had accomplished our mission. I felt the bullet but at the same time the lights went out, the explosion must have knocked out the power station which was next to the base.

The bullet hit my shoulder and I went down as if dead. The torches flashed around, the Germans making sure we were all dead and then they left on the way back to what was left of the base.

I heard the engines of the trucks and waited until there was silence. I dragged myself upright and luckily I still had a torch on me. I looked at my dead companions; I was the only lucky one. The wound was not too bad and the bullet had passed straight through the muscle. I bound up my shoulder with some difficulty and went outside. The mountainside to the South was aglow with red and crimson fire. We had done it but at what cost, I was here alone and how would they know to come and pick me up. I dragged myself up the hillside away from the hut and spent the next day hiding there afraid that the Gestapo would return, but they had more pressing things on their agenda.

Two nights later a small fishing boat came into the inlet.

I was quickly hauled on broad and desperate for food was given something to eat. The Norwegians checked the hut, then poured petrol over the bodies, before setting alight to them, as the ship headed away from the scene. It would be prudent, just in case someone came back to count the bodies, it was also a fitting funeral pyre for five very brave men. Before I told my story I asked to see the Captain of the boat and only told it to him as I feared that someone had betrayed us to the Germans and told them what we were about. It could only have come from one of the Norwegians, either on shore or one of the crew. The captain looked thoughtful. 'I think I know what happened. Wait a minute he said.' He went up on deck and barked some orders. Very quickly one of the crew was tied up and brought below.

'Now Gustafson we have some questions for you.'

'What are you talking about?' asked the man, looking frightened.'

"Why did you ask to leave the boat three days ago and where did you go?"

He looked afraid. 'I went to see my father who is dying, you know I did.'

The Captain looked at him as if searching him inside.

'We can check you know, when I get back to

Shetland I will make enquiries to see if what you say is true and if your story is correct.

Be careful Gustafson we will be watching you, untie him.'

Later that night as I slept Gustafson jumped overboard to a certain death in the cold North Sea.

We returned to Lunna a very sad group, there was no elation in a job well done it was just one of accepting the brutality and sometimes futility of war.

I felt guilty having survived, after a period of recuperation, I was based in England checking and making explosives until the war ended."

Looking him straight in the face Rory finished his last gulp of whiskey.

"That was quite a story, but I don't understand what it has got to do with this ship 25 years later?"

Peter looked him straight in the eyes. "Last night, when I was walking through the ship, I came face to face with one of the Germans on board, I recognised him. It was the Gestapo Officer who interrogated us and killed my five companions."

Heather and Rory looked at each other their mouths slightly open, not able to speak.

It was Peter who spoke. "I don't think he recognised me, after all why should he, he probably thinks me dead. There is something else which I need to tell you, but not now, I have told you enough, you can at least understand how I feel, I need to think for a couple of hours. If you still want to help me, come back later this afternoon."

Heather and Rory carefully left the cabin making sure they were not seen. They went on deck for some fresh air and also to talk.

Rory was first to speak.

"What have we got ourselves into Heather?"

"I don't know." said Heather as she looked out on the beautiful scenery slowly unrolling before them. "What I do know is that Peter needs our help and he trusts us. My father was in the war, he was lucky and came back, he always spoke of the debt he owed to those who never returned and how he could not do anything for them. Maybe this is an opportunity."

Rory gave her a hug. "That's what I like about you, you are brave and not frightened of situations that others would run a mile from."

Heather held him tighter. "Just watch it young man, it has been known for clergymen to fall from cruise ships and never be found again."

They both laughed.

"Come on" said Heather "I'm hungry let's go for lunch." As they came off the deck, they passed the hot tub, occupied by the four Germans and this time both Heather and Rory both winced as they walked passed them.

Lunch consisted of 'Blomfaalsuppe' a cauliflower soup with dried ham and freshly baked Norwegian countryside bread. They were not going to have a sweet until they saw the 'Matha's Knipe' a classic Norwegian farm desert, with blueberry coulis.

After lunch the boat was in Alesund for a couple of hours. Heather and Peter decided to act normally and go on the walk around the town accompanied by the local guide. It was very interesting and Rory approved of the local custom of restricting alcohol and only allowing it to be sold from one venue in each town, because it was so expensive it reduced the problems Norway had with alcohol compared with other countries.

When they got back on board they went up on deck and watched the boat navigate into one of Norway's most beautiful fjords Hjorundfjorden, 33 kilometre long and one of the most idyllic and beautiful of the scores of fjords they would experience. Beautiful as the scenery was Rory and Heather's thoughts and conversation kept drifting back to Peter and his story. Standing on the deck they felt enveloped by the sea and the mountains, raising their eyes to the stunning jagged peaks of the Sunnmere Alps, Peter's story of war, espionage and traitors seemed far, far away.

The further you went into the fjord the narrower it became, small farms clinging to the steep terrain as the mountains slope steeply from the sea. You could feel trapped and hemmed in, not unlike what Peter must be feeling at the moment thought Heather.

When the boat turned around and headed back up the fjord they decided to go and see Peter. They knocked on his door but there was no reply. Immediately they feared the worst and began looking around the ship for him. Just as they thought he had disappeared they found him, in a small lounge on the top deck which they hadn't noticed before, he was tucked into a corner reading a newspaper.

"Peter, we thought we had lost you."

"I needed to get out of the cabin, I thought why should I hide, I am not a criminal I have done nothing wrong". They all agreed, but they had to be careful.

Heather asked the question which Rory had

thought of asking but had not plucked up the courage.

"These Germans, if you have recognised one of them, what are they doing on the ship? Where are they going? Also, it's an odd group four men by themselves, what kind of party is that?"

Peter thought for a few moments then looked at Heather. "I was right to confide in you two, you are the right people to take this forward if anything happens to me."

Rory looked anxious. "What do you mean, is your life in danger?"

Peter looked resigned to the situation. "It is now I have seen Herr Enklemann, that's his name. But I notice from the passenger list he is not travelling by that name, probably because he is wanted as a War criminal.

"War criminal?" Heather exclaimed.

"Yes, you don't think what he did to my platoon was an isolated incident. I did some research after the War, he was on the list of wanted Nazi's for war crimes. Our friend Herr Enklemann has quite a list of crimes to answer for. The authorities would be very interested in learning the whereabouts of our German friend."

"Shouldn't you cable the authorities, or even tell the Captain?"

Peter looked composed. "No, not yet, there are other fish to collect in the net."

"What do you mean, the other three Germans?"

"Yes, they are also probably linked to the Gestapo and war crimes but I have something in my cabin which I want to show you after dinner which will explain everything. But I am spoiling your honeymoon, go and enjoy yourselves, I don't want to spoil your cruise."

Heather and Rory went to the front of the ship to sit and enjoy the panoramic view as the cruise ship slipped effortlessly forward through the fjords and spectacular mountains. Heather tried to read a book, unsuccessfully as her mind kept going back to the story Peter had told them.

Rory quickly dozed off next to her and she was left to ponder what the evening would unfold and what further surprises Peter had in store for them. Well, at least this was a honeymoon to remember!

Dinner was uneventful. Peter was much more assured and even joked with everyone, pulling Cara's leg about Americans abroad and how they expected everything to fit their needs. Cara was having none of it and gave back as much as she received, it was good fun and if it wasn't for the dark shadow of Peter's earlier story it would have been quite a memorable time at dinner.

Rory and Heather waited half an hour before going to Peter's cabin. Again they were careful to make sure no-one saw them enter the cabin. They found him already seated with a package in front of him; there were three glasses and a bottle of whiskey.

"Please be seated, I have something to show you, but first join me for a drink?"

He poured three glasses and then placed the parcel in front of him. It was about 16 inches long and about four inches thick. It was wrapped in black cloth. Peter unwrapped the cloth and a book appeared from beneath the wrappings. The book was hand bound in black goatskin leather, tooled in gold leaf on the spine and front board. Unfortunately, it had also been damaged by the look of it in a fire.

Tooled on the front in gold was the insignia of the German Gestapo.

"Do you remember I told you I was an antiquarian bookseller?

"Yes" said Rory. "But is that true after all you have told us?"

Peter smiled, "Yes it is, after the war I settled into a little bookshop with my wife in an Oxford village buying and selling second-hand and antiquarian books. We did quite well; she died by the way about five years ago. I bought collections from collectors and also at auctions. Two years ago something very strange came my way. I was asked to value a collection before it went for auction. It was from a Jewish man who I had known for many years, he specialised in books about the Second World War. It was quite a collection, it took me three days to catalogue and value the books. The auctioneer asked how much my fee would be. I said, could I take a few books in exchange for the fee. There were a couple of first editions of Wilfred Owen poems, one with an inscription, there was also something else, I wasn't sure what it was but I did think it was so unusual it deserved closer scrutiny.

I showed him the valuations and said I would be prepared for him to ask another dealer to value the Wilfred Owen books so that I wasn't taking undue advantage. He told me it would not be necessary as he trusted me.

The auction took place and I even bid for some of

the books. It attracted quite a number of overseas collectors and the auctioneer told me later he had been asked if that was all the books in the auction from the vendor. He had said yes, he had not disclosed my involvement, why should he, it would make him seem not to know his business if he had to bring someone else in to value and catalogue the collection.

Then something sinister happened. After the auction there was a break-in at the auctioneer's premises, nothing was taken, just a break in. A few days later I noticed that there had been a break in at the address of the collector who had died. Again it was said there had been nothing taken.

I was beginning to feel uneasy and started to examine this book. My German isn't very good but it's good enough to recognise what it is. The Germans are nothing if not meticulous something which let them down after the war as they kept such detailed records, even records of the trains going to the Concentration Camps. Evidence, which years later would be used against them. I quickly realised that this book was a record of a meeting in Liltr Rovan Norway. It is the record of who was at that meeting and a promise to meet again every ten years. Peter turned the book towards Rory and Heather and showed them the pages filled with names written in thick black ink in old German gothic script recording the meeting. This year in the month of September, the meeting is due to take place on the 13th of the month. Today is the tenth. In three days' time they will assemble again in Liltr Rovan"

Heather looked amazed, "Let me have a look, I

used to teach German." Heather pored through the journal as Rory took another gulp of the whiskey.

"But why haven't you handed it over to the authorities? If it is a list of the Gestapo in Norway and if those alive are going to meet again in three days' time, the police have to be alerted."

Peter smiled. "As soon as you do that my friends, they will all disappear. How do you think they have managed to escape the allies after the war and kept hidden for so long, just by luck? No, they have friends in high places, who both protect and warn them. Remember that during the war not all Norwegians were on the side of the allies, there were quite a number who sided with the Germans."

Heather looked up from the book. "What's this list, I can't read it, is it in some sort of code?"

Heather was pointing to a list of what looked like names but they are in some sort of code and not easy to decipher.

Peter looked at the page. "Yes I think it is, it is a list of the Norwegians who helped the Gestapo, those who escaped justice and no-one knew that they were collaborators."

"But what are you intending doing?" asked Rory. "I still have trusted friends in Norway, I am meeting them at Tromsa, we are going to the meeting place and I have a few surprises for them."

Heather looked at him in panic. "You're not going to blow them up are you? You have the explosive knowledge."

Peter smiled trying to reassure them. "I have come for justice, my Norwegian friends want this, they want to expose these people, they want a trial and show them up for what they are."

Heather breathed a bit more easily. "Thank goodness for that."

Peter smiled. "At one point I wanted to blow them up but the Norwegians persuaded me against it, anyway it is not easy to smuggle explosives on board a cruise ship."

"I'm relieved about that." said Rory.

He returned to questions about the book.

"How on earth did it end up in England?"

"I'm not sure. I think it was held in Norway by one of the people named in the book. Somehow, someone got hold of it and it got in the hands of the Jewish collector in Oxford. Maybe someone was trying to expose them. I don't know. The book holds one clue though. Turn it over and look at the back."

Heather turned the book over and the leather was badly scorched and it had obviously been in a fire.

Peter looked at them both. "There are two things very common in Norway, fires and books. Buildings are often made of wood and there are open fires. The Norwegians also love books and read a lot. I can only presume that this book was rescued from a fire and was then passed on till someone recognised what it was."

"But what about the Jewish collector, surely he would know what it was?"

"Yes, I think he did, I did a bit of research after I got the book and learnt that our collector friend had been doing research in the local libraries, especially about Norway and the Second World War, I think he was on to it but died before he could complete his research."

"Was his death suspicious?" asked Heather.

"For once I don't think so, he was 87 and in poor health. He died from cancer after a short spell in a nursing home."

"Do the Gestapo know the book is missing?"

"I don't know. The break-in at the collector's house and also at the Auction house would suggest someone suspects something. Someone is looking for the book. In a couple of days they will definitely know when it does not show up at the 10th anniversary."

Heather looked puzzled. "But why record something that is so dangerous?"

Peter shrugged his shoulders and Heather noticed him wince slightly, the war wound must still hurt.

"That's the German method. They want to record things in their own meticulous way. They have put the Norwegians in code which would suggest they know the importance of that information. The names of the Gestapo are well documented and they have all changed their identities anyway and probably some their appearances."

Heather looked at Peter. "What are you going to do at the re-union if you weren't going to blow them up?"

Peter smiled. "We are going to record who is there, we need to recognise a couple of the Norwegians in order to crack the code. Once we have done that and seen them up close, we will alert the authorities and hand them over to them. That's where my friends from Norway come in. They have had their suspicions over the years but no proof, this meeting will give them the proof they need."

As they stood up to go Heather turned to Peter, "I

hope you keep that book safe, do look after it."

"Don't worry" said Peter "it is my most precious possession"

That night Heather and Rory went to their cabin early and cuddled up close in their double bed. Both of them had an uneasy night going over the story they had heard from Peter and it wasn't just the rolling of the ship in the storm that made a disturbed night for both of them.

DAY THREE...Trondheim to Torvick

The next morning at breakfast it was two rather silent figures who sat at the table looking out at the beautiful vista that lay before them, but they were not noticing the scenery, they were preoccupied with their own thoughts, going over in their minds the incredible story Peter had told them. They didn't really concern themselves with the food, they just ate automatically. Rory reached over the table for Heather's hand.

"Look I don't want all of this to spoil the holiday, you shouldn't let it worry you."

Heather smiled. "I'm not worried about myself, I'm concerned about Peter and what he has got himself into. He has confided in us and we have a responsibility to help him. Anyway I'm up for it as long as you are, you're not backing out are you Watson"

Rory realised at that moment why he loved Heather and why they had married, her courage, her love of life, and adventure. Life would never be boring and yes, she was right. Peter had come their way and deserved their help.

Rory looked at Heather. "Are you going to ditch your valuable assistant Sherlock?"

"Only if he is a wimp." They both laughed and continued with their breakfast. As they were finishing and about to leave, the four Germans came in and sat down at the other side of the dining room.

Rory looked at Heather. "If only we could find out a little more about them, what they are talking about, if they mention Peter or give us any clue. But they are always speaking German."

"I know" said Heather rather coyly. "I have been thinking about this as well. You know that I taught German for a couple of years, it's a bit rusty now but I understand the basics and I have had an idea.

The last couple of days they have used the hot pool on the deck in the afternoon. I could go and join them and pretend I don't understand what they are talking about."

Rory's eyes widened. "You wouldn't do that would you?"

"Well, I won't be at any risk. It's a public place, they are not going to do anything."

Later that morning, they passed the Landegode Lighthouse, built to highlight the dangers to shipping of the chain of islands, with their sharp peaks rising out of the ocean. There would be no human lighthouse to warn Heather of the dangerous waters she would be entering when she entered the pool later that day.

They both sat up on deck where they could see the hot pool. Just after lunch, like clockwork, one of the Germans came up to the pool and felt the temperature of the water. He gave the thumbs up to his friend. Heather jumped up and said to Rory,

"Now they are going in, I'm off to get changed to see if I can be in before them."

She put the two swimming costumes she had brought with her on the bed, a conservative black one-piece number and the one she had specially bought in a flight of fancy- a white bikini, which was a little revealing and she wondered if she dared wear it in public. While she was undressing she decided, in for a penny... she thought, and anyway I will be under the water most of the time.

She wrapped the towel around herself and went up to the top deck. She began walking towards the pool. Her heart sank as she turned the corner behind the large funnel and saw the pool. There they were, three of the Germans, the rather large one, Herr Enklemann and the two thinner ones.

They looked at her as she approached the pool.

"Can I come in?" she said hesitatingly.

Two of the men made room and smiled. "Fraulein, yes by all means, please come and join us."

Their eyes never left her as she let the towel fall onto the floor and gingerly step into the hot tub. She now wished she had been wearing the black swimming costume, but now it was too late.

She quickly stepped into the pool grateful that her body would be covered by the water. She put her head under the water so they wouldn't notice her blushes.

Then one of them smiled at her and said "Sprecken si deutsch?"

Heather looked vacant and held up her hands as

if to say no.

They then started talking quickly in German and laughing.

Occasionally one of them would speak English and include her in the conversation but mainly they spoke German, little realising that Heather could understand almost every word.

They talked about the cruise and how much they were enjoying it, how good the food was. They also commented on her figure and she got quite hot when one of them said what he would like to do her not realising she could understand every word. Again she had to duck under the water to hide her blushes.

Then the fourth German arrived and slipped into the water nodding to Heather and one of the others told him it was okay to talk, she didn't understand German.

The fourth German then said he had spoken to Silver Fox and everything is alright, everyone is coming and there will be some very special guests. They then talked about football and drinking and nothing of real importance was said.

Heather decided it was time to get out of the pool, another embarrassing moment she thought.

She smiled at them all and wished them all well – joking that they shouldn't stay in too long, they would shrivel up. She only realised what she had said when she was climbing the small ladder out of the pool and heard the comments in Germans about her figure. She was quite flattered in a way that she could still have such an effect.

She picked up the towel and wrapped it around herself before smiling again and waving at the Germans and running off, back to the cabin.

Rory was waiting for her. She burst into the cabin dripping wet and Rory held her in his arms

"Was it so awful love?"

"Yes," she said " but I had to do it. Rory, make love to me."

She quickly stripped off her bikini. It would be another hour before they both left the cabin for a walk around the deck before dinner.

Peter was not at dinner but they saw him while they were having coffee afterwards in the bar.

He came up to them and asked if he could come to their cabin later.

Heather and Rory were lying on their bed reading when there was a light tap of the on the door.

Peter came in rather furtively carrying a bag which obviously contained the book.

They gave him a drink and he sat down eager to hear the news of the afternoon. "What did they say, how did you manage to understand them if they were speaking German?"

Heather explained that she taught German for two years and could understand the language.

"You must tell me everything they said".

Heather blushed slightly, "Well a lot of it was comments about my body but when they got over that it was all about food and drinking and football. Oh! and there was something I couldn't understand about a Silver Fox."

Peter looked apprehensive. "What was it about the Silver Fox?"

Heather looked puzzled. "That's what I couldn't understand, it was when the fourth German came in and joined the others in the pool I think he said he had talked to the Silver Fox."

Peter now looked troubled, "Did they say anything else? You must remember everything they said."

Heather tried to remember. "Something was said later on about everything going well and that they are all turning up. Oh yes, and there will be some very special guests."

Peter look agitated. "This is worse than I feared. If Silver Fox is on board it now means I am in great danger if news about the book and my connection with it reaches them." Peter clasped his hands together.

Rory looked puzzled. "What is this about a Silver Fox? Could they mean they could have seen one on land?"

Peter smiled. "If only it was that simple. During the War, in Norway there were many Norwegians who supported the Nazis and what's more they were prepared to betray their neighbours, members of their community and even sometimes their friends. That's where the term Quisling was first used, here in Norway. One of our politicians Vidkun Quisling who started the Norwegian Nazi party, gave his name to mean betraying his fellow countrymen. After the War many collaborators were tried and others killed but some just continued on with their lives. In the book there is a list with 14 names. They are all animal names and Silver Fox is number one. These names are in code because to reveal them would mean death to the individuals. If the Silver Fox is on board then I am great danger, we don't know who he is. It could be one of the crew, one of the stewards, even the Captain himself."

They all fell silent, not knowing what to say.

It was Heather who broke the silence. “Let’s review what we have learnt and Peter you must be completely open with us, do not keep anything back if you want us to help you.”

Peter looked fearfully at both Heather and Rory. ”You have done enough, I can’t involve you anymore in something which could be very dangerous and you don’t have to get involved in.”

Heather looked at Rory before replying. “Rory and I can make our own decisions. You need help and we are here. We want to help you Peter and we know the dangers.”

Rory took a gulp of whisky wondering if they did know what they were getting into.

Peter looked re-assured. “I have told you most things except one. I have been in touch with some of my old friends in the Norwegian resistance. They are meeting me at Tromsa. We are then going to the meeting place for the 30th anniversary meeting of the Gestapo and the Norwegian Quislings. On the Friday we are going to photograph who goes in, especially the Norwegians, and find out who they are. We believe there are some pretty big names involved and they have been protected for a number of years. We will then inform the authorities and expect them to move in early on the Sunday morning.”

Heather asked. “Why can’t you tell the authorities as soon as you can so they can be ready for the gathering?”

Peter had a wry smile. “How do you think they have kept free all these years, they have contacts in very high places. We can only go public when we are sure they are all there and also this book will provide some very damming evidence.”

Rory asked another question. "Peter, you were an explosives expert during the war, can we have an assurance that you are not going to blow them all up?"

Peter looked him in eye. "I must admit, it did go through my mind, but no, that is not the answer, these people need to answer for their crimes, especially to their fellow Norwegians."

Heather looked at both of them. "What are we going to do before Tromsa, it's three days away."

Peter answered. "We keep a low profile, keeping an eye on the Germans but not drawing attention to ourselves. It would help if I could hide this book. If they do suspect me or have made a connection with the auction house then they will be on the lookout for this book. Also, if Silver Fox is a member of the crew it means they have access to pass keys and can get into all of our rooms."

"I hadn't thought about that" said Heather.

Peter clasped the book to himself. "I don't want to leave it anywhere but it's too dangerous now to keep in my cabin. Also, if they are watching they will have noticed my dinner companions."

Heather thought for a few moments. "Yes, you're right, you stay here with the book and Rory and I will look around the ship and find a suitable hiding place, one we can keep an eye on that no-one will suspect."

"A tall order Sherlock." Rory said wryly. Peter looked puzzled at the reference to the detective.

Rory and Heather left Peter in their cabin telling him to lock the door and they would use their key to get back in.

They went to the main deck and started looking

around. It would not be easy, there was little cupboard space anywhere and if there was a cupboard then it was too obvious. There was nothing under the seats and it was proving harder than they had thought. They went through all the public decks and came up with nothing really suitable. They went down to the bar and had a drink to have a talk before returning back to the cabin.

They noticed the Germans laughing and drinking and when they saw Heather lifted their glasses to toast her. She blushed slightly dreading to think what they were saying to one another. Rory and Heather sat down with their drinks watching the pianist and the people on the dance floor.

Then Rory exclaimed. "I have it, the perfect place, it's staring straight at us, but we will have to wait till after the bar has closed to hide the book."

Heather frowned. "What are you talking about Rory? I can't see anywhere, it's too open with the number of people who are here."

Rory leant closer to her. "Look at the music speakers for the pianist. They are massive and will be hollow inside. There will be plenty of space inside one for the book. With everyone in the bar most of the day and evening it's the perfect place, no-one will think of looking here."

Heather smiled and gave him a wink, clinking their glasses together.

When they returned to their cabin they let themselves in and found Peter sound asleep clutching the book, on top of the bed. He was very apologetic saying he hadn't had much sleep the night before, worrying about everything. He agreed that the music speakers would be a good hiding place and he entrusted the book to Heather and Rory before retiring to his cabin for what he hoped would be a good night's sleep.

At around 12.30 Rory and Heather left their cabin and with Heather carrying the book under a blanket made their way to the bar. There were some people just leaving and then the bar was empty.

Heather kept watch as Rory went over and examined the speakers. He pulled out his Swiss Army knife and started unscrewing the back of one of the speakers. Sure enough there was enough room for the book and after placing it there, screwed the casing back.

They returned to the cabin as the ship began it's entry into another little port and the delivery of passengers and goods.

DAY FOUR...The Arctic Circle

The following morning was bright, clear and very cold. Heather went for a jog around the deck before breakfast, Rory stayed in bed a little longer.

She came back to the cabin breathless and pushed a snowball into Rory's bed. He shot up, shouting and complaining loudly.

"Don't be a wimp" said Heather laughing. "You need to be up and about to enjoy the best of the morning."

As Heather was having a shower and Rory shaving he suddenly put the hot tap on full at the sink. It was only a few moments before there was loud shriek from behind the curtain and then Heather pulled it open and threw a wet sponge at him.

"Touche" said Rory laughing.

Again breakfast was divine with a vast array of food. They sat with Cara and enjoyed hearing about the fun she had on some of her cruises.

Soon after breakfast the ship docked at Sandnessjoen and it was the day for an excursion and an Arctic dog sled ride. Peter stayed on board, he said he wanted to read a book and went into the bar where he could keep a good eye on his treasure. Rory and Heather went on the excursion and greatly enjoyed hurtling through the Norwegian forest on a sleigh pulled by huskie dogs. It was a thrilling experience.

They returned to the ship for dinner and found Peter still there reading a book in the bar, the music had begun and there were quite a few people gathering there. They told him about their day and everything seemed so normal, just like a holiday on board ship should be. The ship gave a loud blast and was on it's way once again. There was an announcement that a storm was forecast for later, so the ship may well have to navigate some very rough waters.

Just before dinner they crossed the Arctic Circle which meant a ceremony on the top deck. Some of the crew were dressed in what looked like Viking costumes and if you were adventurous enough to undergo the ceremony of having iced water poured down your back you were rewarded with a tot of vodka. Needless to say Heather was first in the queue and the ship's crew delighted in pouring ice-cold water with ice-cubes down her back. Rory couldn't believe it when she took her place at the back of the queue for another turn. Would he ever work that women out he thought?

Dinner was uneventful. Peter seemed a bit

brighter and started talking about his love of books and some of the stories associated with antiquarian book dealing. Rory told some stories about the clergy he had known and they enjoyed a great dinner, not realising that this would be their last on board with all four together.

After dinner Rory and Heather retired to their cabin for a rest, before going to the bar to hear the pianist. They were not in their cabin long when there was a loud knock at the cabin door, it was Peter and he was very agitated,

"Can I come in? I have had a great shock."

Rory poured him a brandy and handed it to him. "What's the matter? You look as if you seen a ghost."

Peter held the glass tightly. "I was walking down one of the corridors, I had gone up on deck to watch the sunset. One of the Germans was coming towards me. It was a narrow corridor, he looked at me when he went past and I thought he recognised me. He looked very strangely at me."

"Who was it?" asked Heather.

"The Gestapo Officer Herr Ennklemann, who all those years ago had shot my comrades and even put a bullet in me."

Heather sighed. "How could he recognise you, he thought all of you were dead."

Peter looked into his glass. "It may just be me, but he looked closely at me, they may be looking for the person with the book, the trail from the book auction may not have gone cold. They may have come back after the killings on the beach and counted the bodies. They were burnt but if they were suspicious they could have worked out the number of burnt bodies and the fact that one was missing."

"What do we do now?" asked Heather.

Rory thought for a few moments. "It's only two nights before we get to Tromsa, if you don't mind being careful you should be okay. Just try and avoid the Germans."

Peter took another drink. "It's not just them I'm worried about. It's the Silver Fox and we don't know who he is?"

They all sat in silence for a few minutes before it was agreed that they had to go on as before. Rory saw Peter back to his cabin with nothing eventful happening.

Rory and Heather did go up to the bar for a drink. The Germans were there and as there was a table next to them they went to occupy it.

They all acknowledged Heather and offered to buy them both drinks. They accepted. Nothing unusual happened and Heather noted that they said nothing out of the ordinary except commentating on her bust and her figure in German and what a lucky man Rory was!

They both looked at the speaker standing on the floor and hiding the special book. If only, they thought, the Germans knew what it was hiding!

The weather did change and the boat had a distinct roll as it ploughed through the waves. Rory and Heather decided on an early night going back to their cabin rather unsteadily, not because of the drink but the movement of the boat as the sea was now getting quite rough.

They both spent a very uneasy night with not much sleep partly because of the ship rolling in the waves but also the uneasiness of what lay ahead at

Tromsa.

DAY FIVE...Ornes to Harsted

The following morning the sea was calm and placid, it seemed hard to believe it had only been a few hours since the storm of the previous night. Everyone seemed to be having a late breakfast in the large dining room. Heather and Rory ate together at a widow table watching the sea slip by and the vista of the hills topped with snow on the rugged coastline.

The Captain then steered the boat through Raftsundet, a 20 km long strait which forges miraculously through the rock between Versterlen and Loftoten. Rory and Heather went out on the deck and marvelled at the way the large boat could navigate between the sheer cliffs the peaks towering 1,000 meters above them.

Later that morning the ship pulled into Harsted Harbour.

Rory and Heather decided on the excursion exploring the small community. Cara was also there on the excursion. Pretty terraced buildings led up from the Harbour against a backdrop of forests and mountains. They enjoyed the morning exploring the older buildings in the town and the large imposing Trondenes Church. They were most interested in the historical centre of the town and the memorial to 800 Soviet prisoners of War. There were also details of the German occupying forces who had built a large coastal fort near the towns well as the 'Adolf Gun' with it's 42cm shells. One of the empty shells was there on display, it looked a fearful size.

They were back on board for lunch and Heather and Rory went together to the dining room. There they found an anxious looking Peter who had obviously been waiting for them. He looked worried and quickly told them his concern. He had been in the Upper Lounge all morning and had gone back to his room just before coming in here for lunch. He was sure someone had been in his room.

Heather tried to re-assure him. "It would only be one of the cleaning staff, cleaning the room and changing the bed sheets."

"No, it wasn't that kind of visit. I know someone has been through my case. It was on top of the locker and I made sure it had the items in it in a certain way. They were in a different order."

Rory thought for a moment. "Couldn't it have fallen off and the cleaning girl putting it back meant that things were rearranged."

"Including this which I found unscrewed." He produced a small cylindrical wooden tube which looked like part of a piece of furniture, it was about seven inches long and made of teak, it was highly polished. He unscrewed it and opened it up to show a collection of notes. It's where I keep my money when I am on a journey – it was open, in my case. I never leave it open. Nothing has been taken. But I know someone was looking for something."

Heather held Peter's hand trying to reassure him,

"I think it may have worked loose, you may not have tightened it properly." Rory said trying to re-assure him.

Peter shook his head. "I know you are trying

to help, but I think they are getting closer and watching me all the time." With that he got up and left the table. About ten minutes later the four Germans came in for lunch and a slight shiver ran down Heather's spine.

Both Rory and Heather went for a refreshing dip in the hot pool on the top deck. They were not disturbed by anyone else and it was rather nice to be immersed in hot water and then feeling the cold air on your face, in the sub zero temperature. After a relaxing sauna they returned to their cabin.

It was while Heather was getting dressed she noticed something about one of the drawers. "You know Rory, you will think me a bit mad but I could swear someone has been through these drawers."

Rory looked up from the bunk where he was reading. "Don't be silly, you are letting Peter's fears get to you. The cleaning staff have access to the rooms and you are just being paranoid with all that is happening."

Heather closed the drawer and thought to herself. 'I know what I feel and I know something is not right. Peter may be right after all.'

The rest of the day was uneventful with Heather and Rory relaxing, sitting in the lounge on the top deck. The fjords and mountains forming a spectacular backdrop as the boat ploughed a slow channel through the ice blue waters.

The boat wound in and out of the fjords stopping off at small harbours and jetties that you couldn't believe a boat that size could get anywhere near.

Dinner was taken with all four of them there although Heather noticed that Peter didn't seem very hungry. Peter and Rory went off to get some coffee in the bar and left Cara talking to Heather. It was then that Cara said something to Heather which made her sit up and pay attention.

Cara leant forward and said "Do you think you can trust the staff on board the ship?"

Heather looked at her enquiringly. "I think so, they are used to looking after tourists, if there were any incidents, it would result in very bad publicity. Do you have any particular concern?"

Cara looked puzzled. "I know the staff come in each day and clean and turn the beds down and tidy up but after I got back at lunchtime I felt rather strange going into my cabin, as if someone had gone through all my things. There was nothing missing so I couldn't say anything but I had the distinct impression that things were not as I had left them."

Heather tried to reassure her and not telling her about her own concerns or those of Peter. She was now convinced that something was not right, Peter was being watched closely and because they were all his dinner companions they too were coming under someone's watchful eye. But who? The four Germans? Or was the Silver Fox on the move?

Heather told Rory her concerns and the conversation with Cara. Rory said there was nothing they could do, just be very careful. He was relieved now they had not kept Peter's book in the cabin and he looked towards the loud speaker which held it's secret, the fifty people in the room unaware of the speakers hidden treasure.

They stayed up late, dancing in the bar and talking to different people. The Germans for once were not there. Neither was Peter.

The sea was a lot calmer during night and both

Rory and Heather had a good night's sleep.

DAY SIX... Harsted to Tromsa

They rose early for breakfast and sat with Cara watching the sunrise over the mountains, the snow peaks lit up with sun and causing multi-coloured patterns and shades on the valleys below.

They had finished breakfast when one of the stewards came to the table with a message.

"Excuse me, I am sorry to bother you but the Captain would like to see you. Would you all please follow me and I will take you to him."

Heather looked at Rory and frowned. Rory shrugged his shoulders. "Perhaps he wants to show us the bridge?"

The steward led the way through doors and passages they had never been through before as these were the crew's quarters. They went up in a lift three floors and came up to what looked like a boardroom. The Captain was standing behind a large table talking to two other members of the crew and someone who was dressed in a white coat."

A tall bearded man of angular features the Captain was an imposing figure. His English was excellent. "Thank you for coming, I am sorry to disturb your holiday but we have a problem which we think you may be able to help us with. Please sit down.

This morning when the crew went on the top deck they found someone in the hot pool. They had I am afraid died, we believe it was your dinner companion Peter"

Cara gave a startled exclamation and Heather

exchanged a worried look with Rory.

The Captain continued. "I know this will be a shock for you and at the moment we don't know how he died but the initial inspection leads us to believe it was a heart attack brought on by the extreme temperature on the deck last night. We would like to know if Peter mentioned any medical condition to any of you and also if he told you he was going to the hot pool last night."

Cara now had a handkerchief to her face and was very upset. "He was such a nice man, we got on so well, he never said anything to me about a medical condition."

Heather spoke up. "I didn't think he ever went in the pool. I am surprised he was there last night. No, he didn't tell us anything about any medical condition."

The Captain spoke again. "We have found some heart tablets in his cabin, also there was an empty vodka bottle by the side of the pool and the Doctor confirms he had been drinking."

Cara sobbed. "I can't believe this has happened. He was fine yesterday."

The Captain looked at Rory. "Because you three knew him best on board ship I would like one of you to identify the body. There will be a post-mortem here in Norway before his body is flown back to England. Would you be agreeable to do it Rev Coverdale".

Rory agreed.

"Then can I ask you to accompany the Doctor to the Medical Quarters."

The Captain turned to Cara and Heather. "Can I offer you ladies a cup of coffee while you are waiting." They both agreed and an orderly came in with two cups as Rory went through a side door with the doctor. While Rory was away they comforted one another and chatted about Peter. The Captain promised them that later in the cruise they could come up to the bridge if they wanted to see the ship come into a harbour.

The Captain said that this was an occupational hazard on cruises with mainly elderly people and this was not the first death on board he had to deal with.Rory followed the doctor through a seemingly maze of corridors and down two ladders. At last they came to a room which was locked. The doctor produced a key and before he opened the door looked at Rory. "I presume being a clergyman you have seen a dead body before". Rory nodded.

He opened the door and switched on the light which was extremely bright. It lit up a room which had various steel cabinets along the walls full of various medicines and surgical instruments. In the middle of the room there was a steel table covered with a white cloth and underneath what could only be a body. The doctor went to the far side of the table and motioned Rory to follow. The doctor pulled the sheet down to the waist revealing Peter, his features white and soapy looking, he looked a little bloated. He was naked except for a pair of red swimming trunks.

The Doctor looked at Rory. "Is this your dinner companion Peter?"

"Yes it is Doctor. Do you know what caused his death?"

The doctor looked thoughtful. "I haven't been able to do any internal examinations, that will be for the post mortem but I have seen this kind of thing before, especially in this country. A weak heart, too much alcohol, a warm hot tub and then the freezing temperature out on deck, a lethal cocktail. The alcohol and the warmth of the hot tub give a false sense of confidence. This has happened before, we should really put a limit on when people can go in the hot tub and certainly not with alcohol.

The doctor looked at Rory who was studying Peter's arms. "What are these?"

He pointed to four marks on one arm, they looked like burns. The doctor looked at them closely and brought a magnifying glass to look at them closer. "I saw them before and couldn't understand them, they look like cigarette burns, did he smoke?"

"I'm not sure." said Rory. "We never talked about it, I never saw him smoking."

"Then it will be for others to decide at the post-mortem." The doctor drew up the sheet but not before Rory had noted the old bullet wound in Peter's left shoulder and something else rather strange which drew his attention, he thought better of saying anything.

They returned to the others in the boardroom. The Captain stood up and thanked Rory for what would have been a difficult task.

"We are contacting the authorities in England and his relatives. Peter's body will be taken off the boat at Tromsa where they will be able to do a full post-mortem and then his body will be flown back to England. I would ask you to be discreet about this with other passengers and not talk about it. The hot pool will be closed until the end of the voyage and at the next port the police will be coming on board to make their own enquiries. I am sure they will want to speak you. I would like to thank you for all help in what has been a difficult time, especially in the middle of your holiday."

The Captain shook hands with all of them and they got up to leave.

They were led back to the main passenger deck. Cara said she wanted to go back to her cabin and lie down. Rory and Heather went into the bar and sat down to have a talk.

Heather spoke first. "What did he look like Rory?"

Rory looked wistful. "Like any other dead body found in water, a bit bloated and two strange things, four marks on his arm which looked like burn marks and his swimming trunks."

Heather looked puzzled "What about his swimming trunks?"

"They were the wrong way round, as if someone else had dressed him."

They both looked at one another each aware of what this meant.

Heather broke the silence. "Peter had no interest in the hot tub, he never went in before and why would he go in at that time of night, it doesn't make any sense. It's preposterous. He must have been murdered."

Rory pondered. "I think he could have been murdered in his cabin –even tortured with the burns on his arms and then taken up to the top deck when everyone had gone to bed. They would have stripped him and put on his swimming trunks and left him in the hot tub with an empty bottle of vodka at his side. They must have made him drink some as well. "

"The bastards." Heather said gritting her teeth.

Rory smiled at her, “Not very ladylike! The one good thing is that they didn’t get the book, they were obviously after that. We have to decide what we do now!”

They made sure they kept together during the day. During the evening they went into the bar and sat listening to the music and staring at the speaker with it’s hidden treasure. It was 11.45pm when the last guest left and the bar staff packed up. Rory and Heather went out into an adjoining lounge. It took the bar staff about twenty minutes to clear up and then they too departed.

Rory and Heather went back into the bar and as Heather kept watch Rory unscrewed the back of the speaker cabinet, recovering the book and then returning as quietly as they could back to their cabin.

DAY SEVEN... Tromsa

In the morning they packed up before breakfast and put the book in a small rucksack which they took along with them to breakfast not daring to let the book out of their sight.

They ate a good breakfast, not sure where their next meal would be or when.

At 10am the ship’s hooter blew and it began manoeuvring into the harbour. Docking took about 15 minutes and Rory and Heather looked over the rail to see who was awaiting them. There was a large black van, obviously to take Peter’s body away. There were also two policemen standing on the quay by themselves and then a group of what looked like passengers who were ready to board. Just a little away from them were a group of people waiting for friends and relatives to disembark.

Heather and Rory made their way to the deck where disembarkation took place. It was crowded with people and as the ship was being tied up people waited patiently for the hatch to open and the ramp to be put down. Something which they had seen two or three times a day happen like clockwork at the different ports.

One of the stewards came over to them. “I think the police will want a few words with you before you leave, your luggage will be taken off and a steward will look after it, perhaps you would like to come this way.”

They were ushered into a small room at the back of the service counter which obviously doubled up as a rest room. After a few minutes two Norwegian policemen came in. They both stood up to greet them

The older one spoke. “Good morning, I am Captain Olafson and this is my companion Detective Svein Erikson, we are very sorry to delay you, it will only take a few minutes, please sit down.”

Both Heather and Rory sat down, the Police remained standing and the younger man took out a note-book.

“We don’t wish to delay you very long, we are investigating the death of Peter Trimble. Did you know him before you met him on the cruise?”

Rory spoke. “No, we met for the first time at dinner on the first day, the ship allocates diners to various tables and we were with Peter and Cara, an American Lady.”

“Yes we will be talking to the American lady.”

"Did Peter complain of being unwell at any time?"

"No he seemed very well, he ate well and never complained."

"Did he mention any illness, or talked about any operations or the like?"

Heather interjected. "No, he seemed quite fit for his age, he was retired and therefore must have been coming up to around 70."

"Quite so." said the Captain.

"When did you see him on the night he died?"

"At dinner, we all ate together."

"Did he drink alcohol?"

"Yes, we shared a couple of bottles of wine between the four of us."

"Any spirits?"

"No, just wine."

"What time was it when you saw him last?"

Heather interjected. "Oh it would be around 8.15 after we had coffee in the bar."

"Where was he going?"

"Back to his room."

"Did he say anything about the hot tub and going in later that night?"

"No, he never said anything about it."

"Is there anything else you think we should know?"

"No." said Rory in a very determined way. "I think we have told you everything we know, we are very upset about this happening, we got on well with him and he was such a nice man."

"Yes, I understand it must be very distressing for you."

The Police officer stood up. "Well thank you, I think the ship will have your home address in England. If we need any further contact where are you staying in Tromsa?"

"The Hotel Bergen."

"A good choice." said the Captain. "Remember to have the kippers for breakfast, they are the best in Norway."

After shaking hands with the officers Rory and Heather were shown out of the room and they went down the ramp, Rory putting the rucksack on his shoulder.

When they got to the bottom of the ramp, the quay was virtually deserted. The black van was backed up against the cargo hold of the ship and they could just see the coffin being transferred. Rory held Heather's hand and they both paused for a few moments watching the coffin being taken off the ship and loaded into the black van.

The steward from the ship was standing on the quay with their luggage and had called a taxi. They thanked the steward who returned to the ship and after loading the luggage Rory asked the taxi driver to wait for a few moments.

Rory looked around. There was no-one. He looked at Heather, it had all come to nothing, what were they to do now? Contact the authorities and that would lead them into more trouble. The police would want to know why they had not told everything they knew about Peter and the book, how on earth were they going to explain that?

Rory told Heather to get in the taxi, he would walk around for a few minutes.

The black van passed him on its way out of the harbour just as the ship's hooter gave a blast to signal it was casting off. Slowly it edged out of the harbour, Rory turned and watched the large ship slowly move away. He turned around and came face to face with a Norwegian man, aged around sixty with a short beard, angular features, casually dressed and he had strong steely blue eyes which seemed to be drilling into Rory.

Rory smiled. “Are you waiting for Peter…?”

The man was silent, looking intently at him.

Rory tried to explain. “Look I know Peter was going to make contact but he can’t, he’s dead.”

The man didn’t blink or betray any emotion but just turned on his heels and started to walk away.

Rory looked after him and in desperation said. “I know about the Silver Fox.”

The man stopped in his tracks and stood still for a few moments, he then turned back to look at Rory.

“What do you know of the Silver Fox?”

Rory knew he had to get this right. “That he is the head of the Norwegian Quislings during the war, that there is meeting planned this weekend at a place not far from here and Peter was going there. He also had a book which you desperately wanted to see. We have that book.”

The Norwegian looked at Rory intently. “How do I know I can trust you. Who are you?”

My name is Rev Rory Coverdale, I was on the ship with my wife Heather on our honeymoon, we met Peter at our dinner table. He trusted us. He was frightened that his secret about the book would be discovered before he could get it to you. He had to tell someone, and he confided in us. We think he was murdered. There were four Germans on the ship and Peter recognised one of them.”

The Norwegian relaxed slightly. “Where are you

staying?"

The Hotel Bergen"

"I will follow the taxi and we will talk at the hotel."

Rory returned to the taxi sweating in spite of the sub-zero temperature. He smiled at Heather. "Your prayers have been answered." was all he said. He told the taxi driver to take them to the Hotel Bergen.

As they got out and paid off the driver they noticed another car draw up and three men and a women get out. They went into the hotel lobby.

Rory and Heather checked into their room and shortly afterwards there was light knock at the door. The four Norwegians were standing there.

"May we come in?"

Rory opened the door wide and they all came in surveying the room and looking closely at Heather.

Rory motioned them to sit down. "This is my wife Heather. Can we get you a drink?"

"Later" said the man who had talked to Rory. "Tell my friends here everything you know about Peter."

Rory told them the full story and all about Peter's death and their suspicions He left the part about the book till the end.

"Peter did entrust something to us which I am sure you are interested in. He opened the rucksack and took out the book still wrapped in the blanket. Very carefully he unwrapped the blanket and lay the book down on the bed. The Norwegians gathered around it and started looking through it talking excitedly in Norwegian.

The older man turned to Rory and shook his hand. "You have done well my friend. You don't know how valuable this book is going to be in the right hands. Here, let us have a drink, you deserve that." He motioned to one of the men to go and order some drinks.

For the next hour they sat in the room together and talked. The older man Gustaf, had been in the Resistance and had met Peter when he came on the raid to the submarine pen. The others were younger and not been in the war but hated the thought of anyone collaborating with the Nazis.

Gustaf gave a toast "To Peter, a very brave man and one who did not deserve to die like he did." They all stood and toasted him.

Heather looked at them all. "What happens next?"

Gustaf answered. "We will take the book and send it to those who are doing the research into tracking down the war criminals and collaborators. It will be quiet safe now, we will take good care of Peter's treasure. You know the Nazi's were foolish. They had this obsession to record everything, write it down, keep it for posterity. It was to be their undoing. This book will be evidence against them and also will give us clues for the ones we do not know."

Heather smiled. "And what of the meeting tomorrow at Litl Rostavatn?"

She saw two of them exchange worried glances. "But Fraulin that is not for you, that is our business, you have done your job and done it very well and we thank you. Enjoy the rest of your holiday, let us worry about Litl Rostavatn."

Heather sipped from the glass of vodka, "Ah, but we do worry, you see those Germans took someone away from us, we would at least like to see them get their just desserts."

"That is out of the question." said Gustaf "It is not possible. We cannot allow it."

Heather looked intently at Gustaf, staring him down. "You said you owe us a debt, this is the pay-off we get to see the finale. What exactly are you going to do at the Chateau?"

Gustaf sighed and looked at Rory. "I don't know about you Reverend, but your wife scares me, she certainly isn't your normal Pastor's wife." they all laughed.

Gustaf went on. "Tonight we are going to the lodge, it will not be, how you say in English, a church picnic, we will have to walk the last two miles over rough country. When we get there we are going to photograph those who come and those who go. That's all. We want to know who is there. Then on the Sunday morning we give the list to the police and ask them to arrest them all. We cannot do it before then as these people have friends in high places. We are the only people who know about this plan. We have someone standing by in the Police who also knows, he is going to alert the authorities on the pretext of a terrorist plot being hatched at the Hunting Lodge by former Nazis. That will bring down enough police, army, and helicopters to cause a frightful stir. They will not be able to leave without being questioned. The press will also be alerted at the same time. We will just melt into the background and produce the book to dam those who have thought they could get away with their treachery and deception for so long."

Heather looked intently at Gustaf. "We also can do something that none of you can do."

Gustaf looked puzzled as Heather continued.

"We could identify the Silver Fox for you. He was on board the ship and he will be at the Chateau. Imagine that, if we can deliver the Silver Fox to you."

Gustaf spoke to the others in Norwegian. He then turned to Heather and Rory. "You are right, you will be useful to us and if you can identify the Silver Fox it would help us, but you have to realise you are putting yourself in danger, we cannot guarantee your safety."

Heather took another drink of the vodka and addressed Rory. "That sounds like a party we wouldn't want to miss would we Dr. Watson?"

They both laughed and the Norwegians frowned not understanding the joke.

Later that afternoon a four by four off road vehicle arrived at the hotel to pick up Rory and Heather. They were glad they had brought a good supply of warm outdoor clothes with them for the excursions from the ship.

Heather and Rory went with Gustaf and the girl Helga.

It took them about an hour to drive out of Tromsa and through the forests onto smaller roads and then onto what was just a forest track. The four-by four made good progress and the little snow that was around didn't slow them up. At last they reached a small clearing with what looked like a mountain cabin with another four by four parked outside.

Gustaf motioned towards it. "This is the advance party, they have been at the lodge all day photographing people arriving, we are to relieve them, we walk from here to the Chateau."

They all got out of their cars and went into the

simple lodge. There were bunk beds and various provisions around the room.

Gustaf packed up the three rucksacks with provisions and they set out from the lodge.

The weather was fine with the sun shining and the snow sparkling on the pine trees in the forest. It could have been the perfect Christmas scene if they had not been engaged in such a deadly mission. They walked for around twenty minutes before they came out of the forest and Gustaf motioned for them to crouch down. They surveyed the scene before them.

There was a small lake partly frozen and just below them perched on the edge of the lake was a chateau, obviously built in former times for important hunting parties or as a mountain retreat. Gustaf had told them that during the war the Nazis had used it as a base for their generals. After the war it had become a private hotel and could easily house fifty or sixty people.

They could see cars parked near the hotel and lights shining from the windows. Gustaf motioned them to follow, carefully crouching down trying to get cover from the shrubs on the sides of the hills.

Eventually they came close to the chateau and there was a movement in the undergrowth ahead of them. A small Norwegian man had crept up the bank towards them greeting Gustaf with a handclasp and then was startled when he saw Rory and Heather.

Gustaf said something to him which obviously re-assured him.

Gustaf then spoke to Rory and Heather, “You stay here with Erling, you have a good view of the side entrance of the chateau, we are going around the front to relieve the others who are photographing the people who are arriving." With that they slid off silently.

Rory, Heather and Erling took up their positions. Erling took out a camera and set up a small tripod. They were about 100 yards from the side entrance where the door led out to a wooden veranda overlooking the lake.

It wasn't long before the door opened and two figures came out and lit up a cigarette. Heather and Rory went cold, not from the snow they had been lying on but the sight of the two figures in black Nazi uniforms. Heather nudged Rory and whispered something in his ear.

She had recognised one of the figures as one of the Germans from the boat. Erling took some photos and they waited watching the men talking and laughing.

Over the next two hours they saw a number of cars arrive at the front door, they couldn't see from their vantage point who got out but they hoped Gustaf and the others were in a position to photograph them.

Heather and Rory were quite cold by now and it was getting dark. Soon they would not be able to take any more photos.

Various people came out for a smoke at this side entrance, women and men who were not in uniform. It was one figure that drew a gasp from both Heather and Rory. A tall distinguished figure in a blue suit, he had a small beard and Rory and Heather had met him before. He was the Doctor from the ship.

Heather looked at Rory and whispered. "He must

be Silver Fox"

Rory looked closely at him, "He is if we don't recognise anyone else from the ship".

When it was dark they heard a gentle rustling and Gustaf arrived with two other Norwegians.

"Right he said. "We are going to the hunting lodge for the night, it is too dark to take anymore photographs, we will be back tomorrow at first light." They all very quietly crept back up the bank and walked the mile or so back to the small hunting lodge in the forest clearing. They quickly got a fire going and all warmed themselves up. They shared a simple meal and Heather told Gustaf about their suspicions of who the Silver Fox was. He agreed it was a strong possibility but they would like to see more of the guests.

While they were preparing the food one of the men was busy developing the films and by the end of the dinner he had developed around sixty photographs. There were around 30 separate people including some of the staff from the Chateau. They were all laid out on the table and each one numbered and all of them gathered around them trying to identify them. Heather could recognise three of the Germans and also the ship's doctor. Others recognised various people and then they consulted a large book which they brought with them comparing the photos and seeing if they could match any of the pictures.

That night around the roaring log fire they drank vodka and beer, telling stories and Rory and Heather couldn't remember a better night they had spent, it all seemed like a dream. The nightmare would come tomorrow.

They went to bed with Heather sharing a small

room with Helga, the other men bedding down in the large room in front of the fire. They had been warned that they would be up before dawn and they would have a very early start.

DAY EIGHT...The Hunting Lodge

It was still dark when Gustaf went round shaking the sleeping bodies and getting everyone up. There was only time for a cup of coffee before they packed the rucksacks with provisions ready to set off before dawn broke.

One of the men was despatched with the photos to drive to Tromsa and spend the day talking to other members of the resistance who would recognise some of the guests at the chateau. Gustaf explained that this was the big day at the chateau with a celebratory meal planned in the late afternoon and the probability of further arrivals.

Heather, Rory and Erling slipped into their former hideaway as Gustaf led the others around to a vantage point around the front. All was dark and there were no lights apart from a couple of lights in the car-park. The moon was out illuminating the lake. Dawn came quickly and with it the first stirrings at the Chateau, fires were lit and smoke curled from the chimneys, lights came on in some of the rooms as people began to stir.

The back door opened and two youngish girls came outside. Obviously catering staff they came out on the veranda for a quick smoke. Over the next couple of hours a trickle of people came out, most of whom they had seen the previous day. Gustaf came over and said things had been very quiet at the front but they were expecting some more arrivals at lunch time. They shared some chocolate and a tot of rum to help keep out the cold.

Later that morning they saw three cars snake down the road and come up to the entrance, there was a bit of commotion as most of the people inside the Chateau came out to greet the cars. Who on earth could this be? Some important person obviously. Rory, Heather and Erling could not see from their vantage point, they hoped Gustaf had managed to take some good pictures. They also noticed something else which filled them with some foreboding. Armed guards had been positioned around the perimeter of the Chateau.

The rest of the morning passed off quietly with the occasional guest or pair of guests who went out for a smoke on the veranda. Gustaf came over looking very excited, you won't believe this who arrived a couple of hours ago, only Henreich one of the most important Germans during the war in Norway. This is going to be quite a coup.

He returned back to his vantage point at the front and they all settled down again for a time of observation and photographs.

It was around 3 o'clock when it happened. Heather felt cold steel against her neck and turned quickly to see a guard pointing his rifle at her, telling her to stand. Two other guards were in similar positions behind Rory and Erling. They motioned to them to start walking to the Chateau. When they arrived they were pushed at gun point into a small room and the camera confiscated from Erling. They were searched for weapons by one of the guards, who seemed to take great pleasure in frisking down Heather. They were then left in the room with one of the guards standing outside the door.

Heather looked at Erling. "What do you think they will do to us?"

Erling looked at them. "I don't know, but I do know we have more to fear from the Norwegians who are here. They will not want to be recognised, they will be afraid to let us out alive."

Rory put his arm around Heather. "Well, you got your wish for the party Sherlock. We have to stay calm and find a way out of this."

They were then taken and put in what looked like a cellar with an iron grilled door, it had obviously been used as a storeroom for beer and lager as drums were stacked against the wall. The guards pushed them down the steps roughly, tied their hands and pushed them into the storeroom.

A guard was left at the door. Heather and Rory lay together in the cell with Erling not far away. After a few minutes the guards returned to take Erling out by himself. One of the others brought some water and bread and cheese and gave them to Heather & Rory.

Heather whispered to Rory. "Where do you think they have taken him?"

Rory drank some of the water. "I would think they would want to question him."

"Do you think they have found the others?"

"Let's hope not, if Gustaf knows we are missing surely he will raise the alarm."

After about an hour Erling was brought back to their prison like cell. The guards threw him in roughly , he was bleeding and his face was bruised.

Before he had time to speak they hauled Rory up and motioned for Heather to stand and follow them. Heather managed to make contact with Erling's eyes which she thought gave the slightest indication of a shake of the head. As they were bundled up the stairs Heather wondered what it could mean. Don't say anything.......about what .....she could only think they not found the others.........certainly they had heard no other noise of people being brought down to the cellars, could they be still out there and free?

They were pushed into the room they had been in before. They blinked in the bright lights as they tried to adjust to the surroundings. Seated at the table was a man in a blue suit, they recognised him as the Doctor from the ship. Standing at the other side were two of the Germans from the boat, both dressed in the black Gestapo uniforms. The large one, Herr Enklemann looked preposterous with his regalia and medals on the front of his uniform.

It was the Doctor who spoke.

"Ah! the English couple, we meet again. Bring them chairs so they can sit down."

Two chairs were placed before the table and they sat down, facing the doctor.

The Doctor puffed on a cigar. "I hope my friends have been treating you well, after all you are on your holiday." His voice changed and became more threatening. "Now tell us all that you know about Peter Trimble."

Rory spoke up. "All we know is that he was killed on board the ship, by these thugs" looking at the two Germans. The large German came forward and punched Rory in the stomach who crumpled up and fell off the chair."

The Doctor looked unmoved. "Now, now we don't need your petty accusations; we are here to discover what you know about Peter."

One of the guards put Rory back on the chair and Heather took a worried look at him.

Heather spoke up, deciding to take a different tack. "Peter was a very brave man, you know he was a member of the resistance. He told us his story about the war, we believe he was coming back for a re-union with his comrades from the war. That is before he was killed."

The doctor smiled. "Ah, Fraulin, a women with a little sense. Thank you. Now, what else do you know? What else did he speak about?"

Heather spoke up. "He told us about this meeting, he said he was coming to observe it, when he was killed we thought we would come in his place."

The Doctor leant back on his chair. "Thank you, so you thought you would have a little excursion from the boat, like a sleigh ride or going to see the reindeer." He then thumped his fist down on the table and leant forward menacingly at Heather.

"Rubbish Fraulin, you are both British Spies. Sent here to spy on our gathering, you have been involved with Peter from the start. What do you know about a book which Peter had in his possession?"

Heather looked at him straight in the face. "You mean the Agatha Christie mystery he borrowed from me to read on the voyage?"

The large German came forward and hit Heather across the face with his leather gloves."

Heather winced from the stinging pain and

looked accusingly at them all. "Is that how you are going to treat women in your Third Reich?"

The doctor smiled and put his hands together.

"Just let us suppose you are telling the truth, you are innocents who have stumbled on something too big for you, out of your league. We have a problem of how to deal with you. We cannot ask you to go home and keep quiet about all of this. You are bound to tell someone and eventually someone will believe your outlandish story of a passenger killed on a cruise boat, of Nazi gatherings in the Norwegians woods and want to investigate. You see, we have had our eye on Peter for some time, we knew about his war record, of the missions he undertook and the escape from the beach. We even knew about him coming into possession of that very special book. He would have been mad to have brought it with him –or entrust it to two amateurs like yourselves. Before he died he spoke very highly of you. Of how you were innocents, not caught up in this, he just felt he had to talk to someone about his fears and regretted involving you. He told us the book was still in England and we will continue our search there. We have contacts and friends all over the world."

"I bet you do." spat out Heather.

The doctor smiled. "But what to do now with our two English friends. Take you out and shoot you as spies! Perhaps arrange a little accident here in the forest, a wooden hut burning down, tourists can be so careless about fires in wooden hunting lodges. There are so many fires in wooden buildings in Norway, it is a great problem. We could even include your friend Erling, your bodies will be found. Any investigation will conclude it was a tragic accident. I myself, or one of my colleagues may be called from Tromsa to undertake the Post Mortems.”

He smiled again, this time joined by the Germans. For the first time since she had been in the room her heart had leapt when he had just mentioned, one Norwegian, they hadn’t found the others, they would go and raise the alarm, Erling had not given them away.”

The Doctor again put his fingers together and looked at Heather. “You have come at a very difficult time, our great banquet is held in half-an hour, with special guests and toasts, nothing is going to disturb that time for us. We have been looking forward to it for ten years. We will deal with you tomorrow. Eat a hearty breakfast, you will need it.”

With that the guards got hold of Rory who was still doubled up and then they took hold of Heather, as they led them away Heather turned to the Doctor and said with a note of triumph in her voice. “The truth will come out Doctor, it always does, oh and by the way if you are going to dispose of bodies do make sure you dress them properly. Peter’s swimming trunks were the wrong way round.”

As they were led away she saw the doctor give the large German an accusing stare and as they left the rooms could hear words in anger being exchanged. A little division in the ranks would not be a bad thing thought Heather as they were returned to the cell.

The guards pushed them roughly through the door and Rory fell in a crumpled heap on the floor. Heather knelt over him asking him how he was.

He managed to whisper. “You were wonderful in

there, I am so proud of you. I think I have a couple of broken ribs but I'm not coughing up blood so that's one good thing. It's painful but I can bear it."

Erling struggled over to them to ask how things had gone. They told him they didn't think they knew about the others. Erling said he had not told them, it was going to be him and Peter originally who would do the observation. Heather asked what Gustaf would do when he realised they had been captured. Erling said that they would go back to the hunting lodge, remove all traces from their stay there and go to Tromsa and alert the authorities. He didn't know if they would believe them, the book would help and the fact that two English people were being held against their will. But it was Saturday night, would they wait till morning? Would they arrive too late if their captors were to stage their "accident" of the hunting lodge fire. Heather felt a cold shiver down her spine and cuddled up closer to Rory.

In the next two hours they could hear music from upstairs as the banquet got underway, The guard was still outside the their cell sitting on a small wooden seat.

It was going to be a very cold and long night and then the morning, what then? Being drugged probably and taken back to the Hunting-Lodge and then left there as it burnt down. Their bodies would be discovered and it would be put down to an accident – tourists and a fire in a wooden hut! Heather shivered and then the inkling of an idea came to her.

She motioned for Erling to come over and join them. Heather whispered her plan to both of them and then asked Rory to tear her blouse buttons with his teeth, he looked perplexed but did what he was asked to do. Erling and Rory then slumped down pretending to be sleeping.

After about ten minutes Heather got up and went over to the cell door. The guard who had been half-asleep nodding off jumped up, alert and looking at Heather. Her blouse was now torn at the front revealing a pale blue bra with her breasts spilling out from the top. She pushed her chest out, accentuating her women hood. The guard was not looking at her face when she spoke.

"I need a pee, can I go to the toilet?"

The guard pointed at the metal pail in the corner of the cell which they were supposed to use and the men had already done so.

"I can't go in that." Said Heather. "Any way I will need some help undressing with my hands tied, you could help me."

It seemed to be an invitation the guard could not refuse. He put his gun down and unlocked the cell. The cell door opened and Heather slipped through, before he could lock it again Heather's knee had connected with his groin and her arms raised above her head came crashing down on the guards neck. As he fell to the floor she was quickly joined by Rory and Erling who dragged him into the cell and with the help of a knife they found in his pocket cut the rope tying their hands and used it to tie up the guard and also stuff a hankie in his mouth.

As they doing this this Rory admiringly looked at Heather. "Good work, Sherlock, you should have been a Bond girl or at least audition for the Avengers."

They slowly went up to the stairs with Erling

carrying the gun. The noise of the revelry was getting louder. As they peeked through the door they could see to one side a large ballroom with people talking and eating, on the other side was the hall leading to the outside door. They knew that as soon as they opened the door they would be seen from the ballroom. All they could do was wait to see if they closed the doors of the ballroom.

It was twenty long minutes which seemed like an eternity. Then one of the servants came out and closed the doors, going off in the other direction to the kitchen. This was their chance, quickly and quietly they crossed the hall and went out through the front door. The freezing cold air hit them immediately and Heather realised her torn blouse was giving her little protection against the sub-zero temperatures.

They stealthily crept down the steps and into the car-park which was in the dark. Erling crept around checking the cars and trying the handles. Heather and Rory followed his example, they could see lights from the Chateau and hear music and dancing, obviously everyone in there was having a very good time. Then Rory found a door of one of the large Four-by-Four's open. Erling came round and got into the driver's seat. He then smiled, they had left the keys in, he motioned for Rory and Heather to get to the back of the car and push the car down the small slope to the car-park exit so they wouldn't raise the alarm. The car moved easily across the snow and soon they were 200 yards from the Chateau. Heather and Rory jumped in the front of the large four by four as the engine roared into to life and Erling put it into gear.

They quickly sped away from the Chateau with

Heather looked anxiously over her shoulder to make sure no-one was following.

They had gone about five miles towards Tromsa when they saw a barrage of light approaching them, it looked like some sort of convoy. As they rounded a corner they saw a car blocking the road and a number of soldiers, there rifles raised pointing at them and at the four-by-four. Erling screeched the car to a halt and the soldiers motioned for them to get out and put their hands up. Heather was relieved to see the convoy but mortified to have to walk towards the cars, lights shining brightly with her blouse torn, hands above head and wondering what on earth she looked like. There was a shout from a familiar voice and Gustaf came towards them. The soldiers lowered their rifles as Gustaf embraced each of them as they hurriedly told them their news. He told them to leave the car and get into the one he was in. They clambered in and someone very helpfully gave Heather a jacket to wear. Gustaf told them once they realised they had been captured they returned to the Hunting lodge and then to Tromsa. The authorities were difficult to convince at first, they did not believe their story. They had to go right to the top in the Government and it was only when they produced Peter's book that they began to take note.

The convoy of vehicles wound its way to the chateau and when they were within about a mile stopped. Rory and Heather could see soldiers dis-embarking and moving towards the Chateau on foot, with the intention of surrounding it. After about twenty minutes the cars moved again, this time going at speed and they were tossed around the cabin of the vehicle as the driver drove as fast as he could.

They screeched into the Chateau car park, immediately more soldiers jumping down for the cars and securing the entrancing. By now there were people at the front door looking agitated.

The Police Commissioner, Gustaf, Erling, Heather and Rory followed by more soldiers went up the stairs and everyone was ushered into the ballroom.

The tables had been pushed back against the side of the wall, there were food and drink on them. A band which had stopped playing was seated on the platform and men and women stood around, the women in long evening dresses with jewellery and the men some in dinner suits and some in German uniforms both Nazi and Gestapo.

The Doctor came forward and coolly greeted the Police Commissioner. “So nice to see you Eric, to what we do owe the pleasure of you company, I would have invited you if I had known you were interested in our little gathering.”

The Commissioner looked past him. “We are here to see what is going on, we have had some very strange reports.”

The doctor replied in an oily tone. “As you can see we have a little gathering, a private party, there is no law I believe against that. We dress up a little and celebrate the times past especially the war, it was a good time for some people and we wish to remember it. I don’t think we are doing anything wrong or illegal.” He looked expansively around the room.

The Commissioner was not done.

“I believe you imprisoned these three people, two

of whom are English Citizens."

The Doctor smiled. "Yes we did, we are quite worried about security and had heard that some people who may not approve of us may try to wreck the proceedings and also threaten our lives. These three were picked up in the grounds, I think our security staff could have been a bit rough and I do apologise and would want to make some kind of reparation to them. They did steal a car I believe but we will not press charges."

Heather by now was completely affronted by the Doctor and his explanations. She stepped forward and came closer to him. "We know you are The Silver Fox, Doctor."

The Doctor looked at the Police Commissioner. "I am afraid your English guest is deluded. I am no more The Silver Fox than you are my friend."

Gustaf stepped forward. "One thing we have Doctor are the fingerprints of The Silver Fox, left after a murder of Norwegian resistance fighters. I am sure you will be able to supply your fingerprints so that we can compare them.

For the first time Heather noticed the Doctor flinch and step back. The German Colonel stepped forward. "All this is ridiculous can you take these people away, can't you see how much trouble they are trying to make. We are having a private party."

Heather came forward and slapped the Colonel across his face; he winced and held his face.

In perfect German she addressed him.

"That is for the comments in the swimming pool, I understood every one of your lewd comments, and it is also for the murder of our friend Peter."

The Colonel looked at Heather open mouthed still rubbing

his cheek. "You whore"

The Police Commissioner addressed the assembly of people. "I am afraid we will need to interview all of you and ascertain exactly who are you, fingerprints will be taken to make sure you are not part of the Norwegian Quislings or German Nazis who are wanted by the War Crimes Commission."

Heather and Rory smiled at each other and held hands. The Doctor was backing away towards the window and suddenly pulled a gun from a pocket and took aim at them both.

There were two gun shots.

They came from the soldiers standing behind the Police Commissioner as the Doctor fell down dead pulling the curtain down he was clutching. There were gasps and shrieks from around the room.

The following few days Heather and Rory stayed in Tromsa at the hotel Bergan. They watched the news on the television as it disclosed the capture of various war criminals and also members of the Norwegian collaborators. They were visited at the hotel by many people including the local Mayor who thanked them personally and also members of the British Embassy.

After three days they were ready to return home. They once more went to the Harbour to board the Coastal Express boat. As they boarded they were surprised to be met by the Captain and the crew who saluted them and thanked them for a great service they had done their country. They were shown into the first-class stateroom and told to enjoy their journey back to Bergan, there would be no expense spared.

As the ships hooter sounded they went to the

rail at the side of the ship and waved goodbye to Tromsa, the small group of brave Norwegians on the shore. Gustaf, Erling, Helga and the others.

Later that evening Rory and Heather relaxed in the stateroom sipping champagne and enjoying the ambiance of the scenery slipping by, their room gave magnificent views over the ship, fjords and the coastline.

Rory and Heather talked about their adventure, of how they were sorry for Peter to lose his life but how he would have been proud to know his mission was accomplished and successful. Of how their honeymoon had been not what they had expected.

Rory turned to Heather. “Can I do something to you?”

Heather frowned “What do you want to do?”

Rory laughed. “Can I tear your blouse again with my teeth, I found it very exciting.”

Heather hit him with a pillow as he complained about his sore ribs.

END

If you have enjoyed this book you will enjoy the first book written by Rev Malcolm Lorimer, Saints and Sinners. The first edition of 2,000 sold out but it is available on Kindle.

Twelve stories linked by the theme of clergy and crime. Each story is about a clergyman or woman and their involvement in crime either as the perpetrator, victim or detective. Some of the clergy are good, others weak and some evil. The clergy are from different denominations, Anglican, Baptist, Methodist and one set in a monastic community.

The novel explores questions about good and evil in the context of life and the church, the stories are not linked together and all have separate characters.

The themes of the stories involve, murder, deception, lust, greed, envy, hate and witchcraft, the usual attributes found in the average church congregation!

SAINTS and SINNERS
12 tales of Crime and the Clergy
Rev. Malcolm G. Lorimer

**Coming soon the third detective novel published by Max Books.
Murder on the Ribblehead Viaduct.**

A group of friends take a trip on a steam train on the Settle to Carlisle Railway in the 1960's. One of them is found dead at the bottom of the Ribblehead Viaduct. Is it a tragic accident or were they pushed from the train? Ten years later the group of friends once more travel the line and the truth is revealed.

The book launch will take place on the weekend ~~of 18th / 19th April~~ 2020 at Ribblehead Station. Why not call in for a book and drink a toast to one of the most beautiful of viaducts. More details on the website. www.max-books.co.uk